MEL BAY'S COMPLETE METHOD FOR AUTOHARP® OR CHROMAHARP®

By Meg Peterson

1 2 3 4 5 6 7 8 9 0

PREFACE

In 1881 Charles F. Zimmerman invented the Autoharp, and it has been increasing in popularity ever since. It is our only completely native American musical instrument. It is simple; it is uncomplicated; and its playing technique has been largely un-catalogued. But it is also versatile, and can prove challenging to anyone who studies and fully develops its potential. Thus, in spite of the fact that it grew without nurturing, a wealth of traditional folk music, old time pop, gospel songs, hymns, spirituals, and bluegrass favorites have been enjoyed and passed down from generation to generation through the use of this remarkable instrument.

Everyone can play the Autoharp at his or her own level. Young or old can "mash the button" and stroke; school children can learn basic harmonies and accompany singing; teen-agers can play favorite rock sequences and create unique strum patterns; and professional musicians can perform complicated and exciting melodies or rhythmic accompaniments.

Yes, the Autoharp is simple, but it's also much more! It can be as interesting as you are willing to make it. Experiment with open string plucking, five finger picking, drag notes, or fast banjo rolls, and it will come alive as a solo instrument to take its place in the folk festivals and concert halls of America.

In this book I have gone far beyond the two previous method books. There are newly-created strum patterns and styles never before notated. This is a self-teaching course to be followed step by step, each of the 48 lessons built on the previous one. There are musical aids for those who wish to relate their study to the teaching of music (notation, theory, harmony, transposition, and substitute chords). There are 122 practice songs and many more suggested ones.

The number of possible Autoharp strums is infinite. You can create your own style...communicate your thoughts, feelings, and desires by making and sharing your own music. Hold your Autoharp close to you, and let it speak for you.

I hope this book will open a new world of warmth and joy and creativity for each one of you!

Meg Peterson

Note to teachers:

For those of you who will use this book as a text, it is important to understand that the division of lessons is optional. Some of you will want to spend an entire period on learning to tune. Others will find certain picking techniques too difficult to master in one sitting, or may wish to combine two lessons in one. Be flexible and adjust your requirements to the abilities of your students. And be sure to delve into the wealth of current popular songs and enhance and update your Autoharp repertoire.

2

M.P.

MOTHER MAYBELLE CARTER
(May 10, 1909 – October 23, 1978)

Photo by Mike Carpenter..

    Back around the turn of the century the Autoharp was reputedly one of the nation's most popular musical instruments. Then it went into decline and lost favor. In 1929 only about six hundred were made. The thirties and forties were not much better and the makers often gave thought to ending their production. But the unique sounds of this American instrument had found a particular appeal to musicians in the Appalachians and it was probably this alone which saved the Autoharp from extinction. As the years passed, mountain music, and particularly the Carter Family, became imbedded in the heart and soul of the nation. This distinctly American form of music spread throughout the land and, as it did, the contribution of Maybelle Carter grew with it.

    She showed us all that the Autoharp is more than just a lap instrument; more than just an accompaniment instrument. When she stepped up to the microphones on stage at the Grand Ole Opry, with the Autoharp held high on her chest, and poured out her music, it was inspiring and beautiful.

    Over the years I was privileged to know her. We had great fun swapping ideas for new licks, finger technique, and ways to improve the Autoharp. I learned so much from her and she shared so generously. Music was her life, and like all sensitive musicians, she knew it was a gift to be shared. And it went beyond that talent. She and my husband put their heads together as he developed the original Appalachian Autoharp, an instrument for the kind of folks who would love and play Carter Family music. This was something new—something exciting!

    History should also record that she loved to give Autoharps as gifts to those dear to her. Every Christmas we could look forward to hearing from Mrs. Carter with her shopping list. She was full of news of her family and questions about mine. She was never too busy to chat and to care. And every time she played an engagement near where I live we would receive a warm phone call and an invitation to come on over.

    So, to me, she was more than just a great country singer and a legend. She was also a very wonderful and decent human being. With all my heart I dedicate this book to her. Her gift to us all will live on forever and does not really need my small contribution, but I offer it on behalf of all of us who loved her and her music.

ACKNOWLEDGEMENTS

My sincere appreciation goes to the many performers, teachers, and Autoharp pickers over the years who have shared their skill, experience, and styles of playing with me.

    Special gratitude goes to the following friends and colleagues whose patience, advice, and knowledgeable criticism helped immeasurably in the preparation of this book: Bill Bay, a superb editor, Rosamonde Ritt, L. H. Autry, Rebecca Magill, Jane Beethoven, Carman Moore, Rosalie Pratt, Drew Smith, Dan Fox, and Tennyson Schad.

    Taking pictures of an Autoharp in action would be almost impossible for anyone but the best. That's how I feel about the work of Charlie McCue, artist and friend.

    Finally, special thanks and affection goes to my mother, Grace Noble, who inspired me to persevere, and to my husband, Glen Peterson, who introduced me to the versatile Autoharp and made possible my extensive study of its technique and potential in all regions of this country.

Meg Peterson

COMPLETE AUTOHARP OR CHROMAHARP METHOD CD AND TABLE OF CONTENTS

Photos by Charles McCue

Book Design by Vic Take

TABLE OF STRUM SYMBOLS

/ = Stroke, using previous chord until a change is indicated

∅ = Stroke in the lower octave

∅ = Stroke in the middle octave

∅ = Stroke in the higher octave

↑ = Upstroke

↓ = Downstroke

↑ = Upstroke Arpeggiando

↓ = Downstroke Arpeggiando

∿⟶ = Combined up and downstroke Arpeggiando

T = Thumb		
i = Index finger		
m = Middle finger		
r = Ring finger		
l = Little finger		

P = Pinch

P (T-i) = Pinch using the thumb and index finger

P (T-m) = Pinch using the thumb and middle finger

P (T-r) = Pinch using the thumb and ring finger

P (P-l) = Pinch using the thumb and little finger

P (T-i-m) = Pinch using the thumb, index, and middle finger

(i-m) = Plucking two strings simultaneously with the index and middle finger

(m-r) = Plucking two strings simultaneously with the middle and ring finger

(i-m-r) = Plucking three strings simultaneously with the index, middle, and ring finger

LF = Loose Fist

Br = Brush

DF = Double Finger Scratch

Ⓗ = Hammerin' On

Ⓓ = Drag Note

Ⓑⓢⓛ = Back Slur

R = Rasgueado

RB = Rasgueado Backwards

Sl = Slap

Bl = Blanking Out All Strings

Tp = Tapping

THE RUDIMENTS OF MUSIC

THE STAFF: Music is written on a STAFF consisting of FIVE LINES and FOUR SPACES. The lines and spaces are numbered upward as shown:

5TH LINE ———————————
4TH LINE ———————————   4TH SPACE
3RD LINE ———————————   3RD SPACE
2ND LINE ———————————   2ND SPACE
1ST LINE ———————————   1ST SPACE

THE LINES AND SPACES ARE NAMED AFTER LETTERS OF THE ALPHABET.

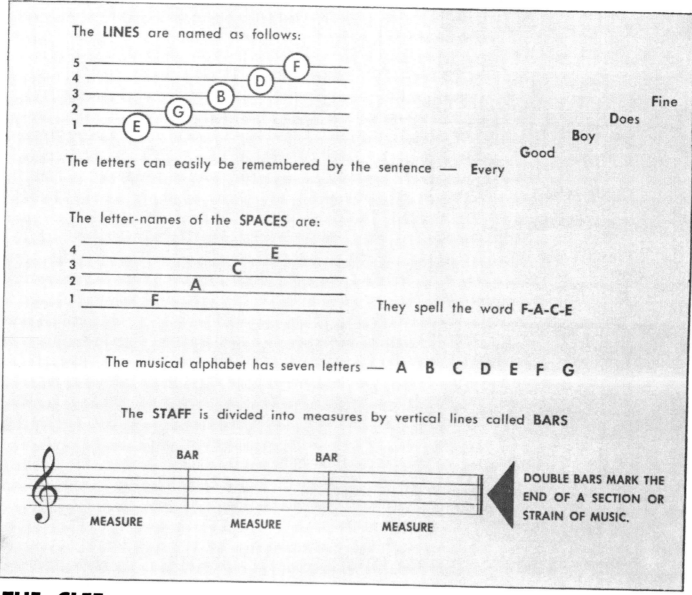

The **LINES** are named as follows:

The letters can easily be remembered by the sentence — Every Good Boy Does Fine

The letter-names of the **SPACES** are:

They spell the word **F-A-C-E**

The musical alphabet has seven letters — **A B C D E F G**

The **STAFF** is divided into measures by vertical lines called **BARS**

BAR   BAR

DOUBLE BARS MARK THE
END OF A SECTION OR
STRAIN OF MUSIC.

MEASURE   MEASURE   MEASURE

THE CLEF:

THIS SIGN IS THE TREBLE OR G CLEF.

THE SECOND LINE OF THE TREBLE CLEF IS KNOWN AS THE G LINE. MANY PEOPLE CALL THE TREBLE CLEF THE G CLEF BECAUSE IT CIRCLES AROUND THE G LINE.

NOTES:

THIS IS A NOTE:

A NOTE HAS THREE PARTS. THEY ARE

The HEAD
The STEM
The FLAG

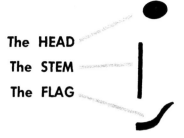

NOTES MAY BE PLACED IN THE STAFF,   ABOVE THE STAFF,

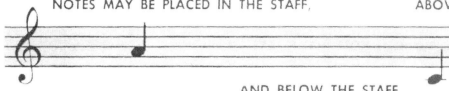

AND BELOW THE STAFF.

A note will bear the name of the line or space it occupies on the staff.

The location of a note in, above or below the staff will indicate the Pitch.

PITCH: the height or depth of a tone.

TONE: a musical sound.

TYPES OF NOTES

THE TYPE OF NOTE WILL INDICATE THE LENGTH OF ITS SOUND.

THIS IS A WHOLE NOTE.
THE HEAD IS HOLLOW.
IT DOES NOT HAVE A STEM.

○ = 4 BEATS
A WHOLE-NOTE WILL RECEIVE FOUR BEATS OR COUNTS.

THIS IS A HALF NOTE
THE HEAD IS HOLLOW.
IT HAS A STEM.

♩ = 2 BEATS
A HALF-NOTE WILL RECEIVE TWO BEATS OR COUNTS.

THIS IS A QUARTER NOTE
THE HEAD IS SOLID.
IT HAS A STEM.

♩ = 1 BEAT
A QUARTER NOTE WILL RECEIVE ONE BEAT OR COUNT.

THIS IS AN EIGHTH NOTE
THE HEAD IS SOLID.
IT HAS A STEM AND A FLAG.

♪ = ½ BEAT
AN EIGHTH-NOTE WILL RECEIVE ONE-HALF BEAT OR COUNT. (2 FOR 1 BEAT)

RESTS:

A REST is a sign used to designate a period of silence.

This period of silence will be of the same duration of time as the note to which it corresponds.

 THIS IS AN EIGHTH REST

THIS IS A QUARTER REST

 THIS IS A HALF REST. NOTE THAT IT LAYS ON THE LINE.

THIS IS A WHOLE REST. NOTE THAT IT HANGS DOWN FROM THE LINE.

NOTES

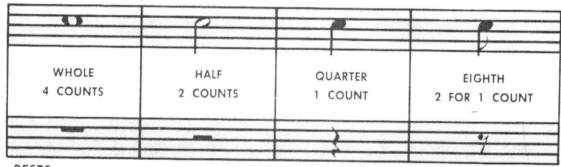

WHOLE 4 COUNTS	HALF 2 COUNTS	QUARTER 1 COUNT	EIGHTH 2 FOR 1 COUNT

RESTS

THE TIME SIGNATURE

THE ABOVE EXAMPLES ARE THE COMMON TYPES OF TIME SIGNATURES TO BE USED IN THIS BOOK.

 THE TOP NUMBER INDICATES THE NUMBER OF BEATS PER MEASURE.

THE BOTTOM NUMBER INDICATES THE TYPE OF NOTE RECEIVING ONE BEAT.

 BEATS PER MEASURE

A QUARTER-NOTE RECEIVES ONE BEAT

 SIGNIFIES SO CALLED "COMMON TIME" AND IS SIMPLY ANOTHER WAY OF DESIGNATING 4/4 TIME.

LEDGER LINES:

When the pitch of a musical sound is below or above the staff, the notes are then placed on, or between, extra lines called LEDGER LINES.

THEY WILL BE LIKE THIS:

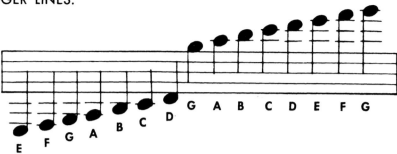

THE TIE

The TIE is a curved line between two notes of the same pitch.
The first note is played and held for the time duration of both.
The second note is not played but held.

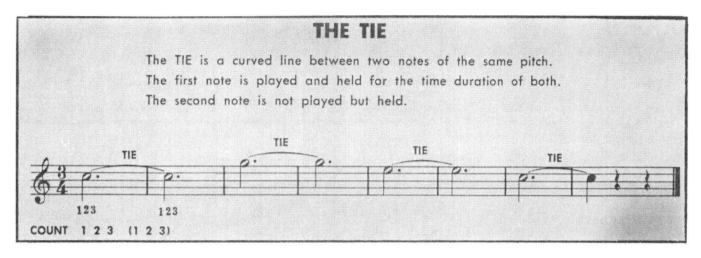

THE EIGHTH NOTE

An eighth note receives one-half beat. (One quarter note equals two eighth notes).

An eighth note will have a head, stem, and flag. If two or more are in successive order they may be connected by a bar. (See Example).

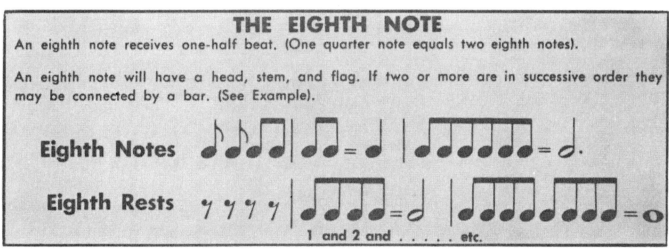

DOTTED QUARTER NOTES

A DOT AFTER A NOTE increases its Value by ONE-HALF.

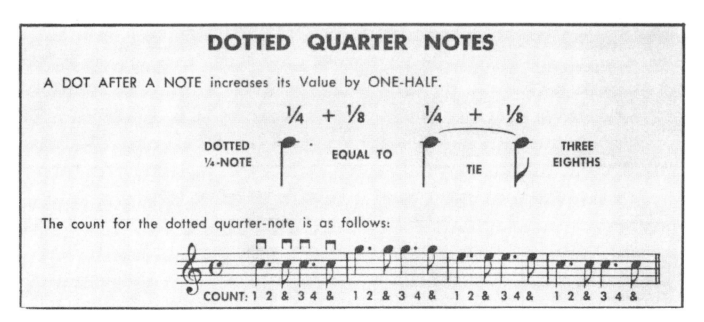

The count for the dotted quarter-note is as follows:

How To Count Triplets

Count: 1 2   1 2   1 trip-let 2 trip-let   1 2

Q. What are TRIPLETS?

A. A group of three notes, played in the time of two notes of the same kind.

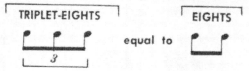

TRIPLET-EIGHTS   equal to   EIGHTS

SIXTEENTH-NOTES

In common time four sixteenth-notes equal one quarter-note.

$$\text{♬♬} = \text{♩}$$

They may be counted in this manner:

1-six-teenth-notes, 2-six-teenth-notes, 3-six-teenth-notes, 4-six-teenth-notes.

Example

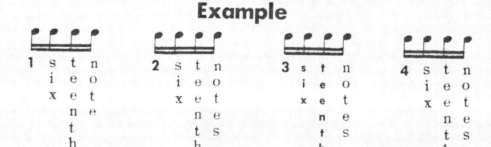

1 s i x t e e n t h   2 s i x t e e n t h   3 s i x t e e n t h   4 s i x t e e n t h
n o t e   n o t e s   n o t e s   n o t e s

TABLE OF NOTES AND RESTS

Whole Note	o	A Whole Measure Rest ▬
Half Notes	♩ ♩	A Half Rest ▬
Quarter Notes	♩ ♩ ♩ ♩	A Quarter Rest 𝄽
Eighth Notes	♫ ♫ ♫ ♫	An Eighth Rest 𝄾
Sixteenth Notes	♬ ♬ ♬ ♬	A Sixteenth Rest 𝄿

In the following, an eighth note is followed by two sixteenth notes.

They may be counted in this manner: 1 & a 2 & a 3 & a 4 & a

REPEATS

DOTS BEFORE AND AFTER A DOUBLE BAR MEAN REPEAT THE MEASURES BETWEEN.

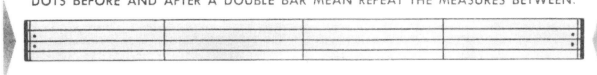

FIRST AND SECOND ENDINGS

Sometimes two endings are required in certain selections . . . one to lead back into a repeated chorus and one to close it.

They will be shown like this:

The first time play the bracketed ending **No. 1.** Repeat the chorus.
The second time skip the first ending and play ending **No. 2.**

OTHER MUSICAL TERMS

Tempo = The rate of speed at which a piece of music is performed.

Syncopation = A musical effect, achieved by accenting an up-beat or a weak beat, giving it emphasis that it would not have ordinarily.

Octave = The distance from one musical tone to the next tone with the same letter name, either higher or lower. In this book, the term will also refer to one of the three sections of the Autoharp (lower, middle, or upper).

D.S. = An abbreviation for Dal Segno, which means "from the sign" ($\%$)

D.S. al Coda = Go back to the sign ($\%$), play to the coda symbol ($\oplus$), and then play the coda.

Coda = An ending section of a musical piece, often symbolized as $\oplus$.

D.C. = An abbreviation for Da Capo, which means "from the beginning."

Fine = The end.

D.C. al Fine = Go back to the beginning of the piece and play to Fine.

LESSON 1: TUNING THE AUTOHARP

The easiest way to tune your Autoharp is to use a well-tuned piano, matching each string to the corresponding note on the keyboard (See scale label in Fig. 2). Be sure to take notice of the correct octave you are tuning and the difference in pitch. A chromatic pitch pipe or any other instrument of fixed pitch (A-440 cycles) can also be used. In addition, a tuning cassette is available which is helpful to both experienced and inexperienced players. It explains how to tune by octaves, by intervals, by the C scale, and by chords. It also tells the player how to change strings.

Stay in tune with
Meg Peterson:
Meg Peterson Enterprises,
33 South Pierson Road
Maplewood, NJ 07040

There is a great deal of stretch in new Autoharp strings as is true of any other stringed instrument. Therefore, the first few tunings will require more time and you will have to turn the tuning pin more revolutions than in subsequent tunings.

As you start, pluck each string and gently lift it with your index finger. At the same time turn the tuning wrench clockwise to raise the string to pitch, or counter clockwise to lower it (In most cases you will be raising the pitch). When the string is in tune stretch it again and pluck it, and you will notice that it will go down in pitch. (Fig. 1) Tune it again, and keep gently stretching until it stays up to pitch. By this time the metal ball on the end of the string will have become tightly "seated" in the string anchor (There is a loop and no metal ball on old "A" model Autoharps strings).

Once the strings are in tune, strum the Autoharp, pressing down each chord bar in turn. This will stretch the strings some more. After a few hours of playing you will find that your Autoharp will stay in tune for long periods of time with only slight tuning adjustments.

It is important that you keep your instrument in a case to insulate it from extremes of heat or cold. Temperature variations affect the pitch of metal strings.

Once the Autoharp tuning has stabilized you will never have to turn your tuning wrench more than 1/8 inch clockwise or counterclockwise. Just be sure you are plucking the same string you are tuning... and not the one next to it! That's how strings get broken.

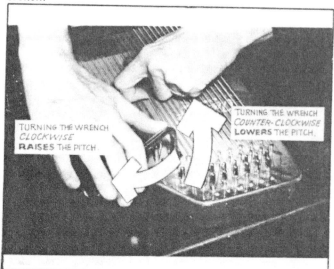

TURNING THE WRENCH CLOCKWISE RAISES THE PITCH.

TURNING THE WRENCH COUNTER-CLOCKWISE LOWERS THE PITCH.

Fig. 1

ABOUT CHANGING STRINGS

It is very important to unwind the tuning pin (turn it counter-clockwise) *several revolutions before replacing a string*. Otherwise, the tuning pin will become too deeply imbedded in the pinblock when you start winding the new string up to pitch.

After removing the old string, slip the ball end of the new string into the string anchor (See Fig. 2) and slide the other end under the chord bars (Remember, Chromaharps and old "A" models have a loop that fits on a small metal peg). (See Fig. 4 p. 12). Make sure it doesn't twist around the adjacent strings. Keeping tension on the string so as not to let the ball end pop out of the anchor, insert about 1/2 inch of the wire into the hole in the tuning pin (Fig. 3). As you turn the pin clockwise be sure the end of the string is under the winding, so it is secure and cannot slip out. Keep the string taut as you wind, pressing down with your index finger to keep the end of the string in place.

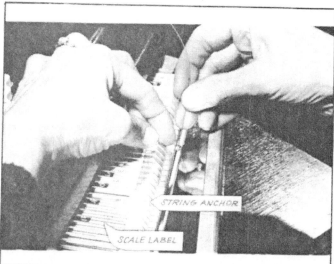

STRING ANCHOR

SCALE LABEL

Fig. 2

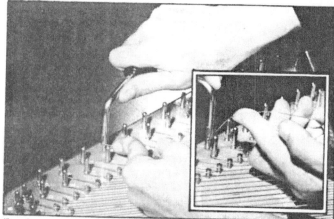

Fig. 3

END PEG

END PLATE

Chromaharp strings have a loop which fits over the end peg. The end plate snaps open for convenience in changing strings.

12   Fig. 4

HOW TO HOLD THE AUTOHARP

Fig. 5

Note the angle of the instrument in relation to the player's body when the Autoharp is on the lap or table.

Fig. 6

As you can see, there are several ways to hold the Autoharp. Most beginners place it on the table as in Fig. 6, then hold it Appalachian style as in Fig. 7 when they become more proficient.

Fig. 7

CHOOSING A PICK

There are four common types of picks used by Autoharp players.

Plastic & metal finger picks

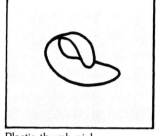

Plastic thumb pick

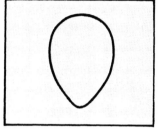

Flat plastic pick

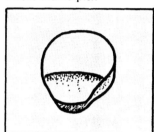

Felt picks

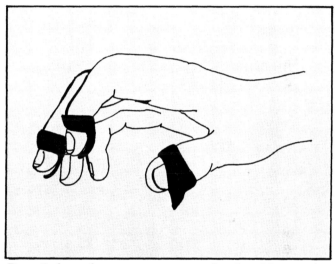

Figure 8 shows the correct way to wear thumb and finger picks. As you become more advanced you will wear finger picks on all your fingers.

Be sure to find a pick that fits snugly, so that it will not twist or fall off while you're playing fast. Metal finger picks come in various gauges and can be bent to fit. Plastic picks have a more mellow sound and can be heated in water until they are soft enough to be molded to the fingers. You can file off the point of the plastic thumb pick with a nail file or emery board to make it rounded for smoother, faster strumming. *Use a thumb pick for the next several songs.*

HOW TO STROKE THE AUTOHARP
Definitions:

A *stroke* is a single motion across one or more sections of the Autoharp.

An *upstroke* ⟋ goes from the lower (bass) to the higher (treble) strings and away from the body.

A *downstroke* ⟍ comes from the higher down to the lower strings, toward the body.

A *strum* is made up of several strokes combined in a rhythmic pattern (discussed in detail on pg. 18)

A *slash* ⟋ represents a "beat" in the rhythm of the piece being played. It also means to continue stroking the chord being used until the chord changes.

13

NOW, LET'S START PLAYING!

Place the index finger of the left hand on the C major chord bar and *press down firmly* (Fig. 9). Use the the thumb of your right hand to stroke the strings to the right of the chord bars......

or to the left about two inches from the chord bars.

Figure 10 requires crossing your right hand over your left, but the tone produced is much richer. The right side can still be used for special effects.

If you are left-handed this is simplified by pressing the chord bar with your right index finger and stroking the strings to the left of the chord bars with your left thumb.

For those who are right-handed and wish no cross-over at all, there is the Attache Autoharp (Fig.11) or the Portaharp built right into a case, with chord bars at the opposite end of the instrument.

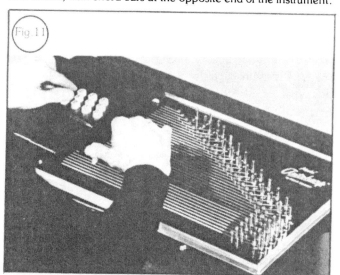

Now, *stroke the strings several times making the instrument ring*. Use a sweeping motion. The wrist should be flexible and the elbow slightly raised. Stroke fairly rapidly to get the full sound of the chord simultaneously. As you stroke, continue the arm around in an imaginary arc until it returns to the bass, or lower, string to begin another stroke.

Be sure to *press only one chord at a time*, holding it down firmly while you are stroking.

Notice how the chord continues to sound when stroked properly. Too heavy a stroke produces a dull sound.

YOU ARE NOW READY TO ACCOMPANY YOUR FIRST SONG

The first song requires only one chord, so press down the chord bar marked C Maj. Remember, the letter (C) above the staff indicates the chord bar to pressed, and each slash (**/**) represents a repeated playing of that chord. Keep a steady beat as you sing and match the strokes to the music. As you count, stroke on both the 1st and 3rd beats of the measure. This pattern of two strokes per measure is repeated throughout the song. Later on, when you have used more chords you may want to add to the harmony.

THREE BLIND MICE

Chords used: C

Three blind mice, three blind mice, see how they run,

see how they run, They all ran af - ter the

farm - er's wife who cut off their tails with a carv - ing knife, did

e - ver you see such a sight in your life as three blind mice.

Since this song required only one chord, you can use any other single "major" chord you wish for practice.

There are several other one chord songs for beginners. Try any of the following songs in the major key of your choice. 'Frere Jacques" (Brother John), "Row, Row, Row Your Boat," "Hot Cross Buns," "Little Tom Tinker," and "Kookaburra."

The following songs can be played using one of the minor chords; Gm, Dm, Em, or Am. "Zum Gali Gali," "Hey, Ho," Nobody Home," "Old Abram Brown," "Erie Canal," "Canoe Song," and "Shalom Chaverim."

LESSON 2: CHANGING CHORDS

Let's try a two-chord song. Use the middle finger of the left hand to press the G7 chord bar. Practice changing from C to G7 several times, coordinating the pressing of the chord bar with the stroke of the right thumb. Do not anticipate a chord change. *The stroke and change must be done simultaneously.*

Locate all chords needed before starting a song. It is helpful to write them below the title like this:

HE'S GOT THE WHOLE WORLD IN HIS HANDS

Chords used: C&G7

He's got the whole world in His hands, He's got the whole world

in His hands, He's got the whole world in His hands, He's got the whole world in His hands.

Repeat each first line two times.

2. He's got the little bitty baby in His hands. He's got the whole world in His hands.

3. He got you and me brother, in His hands He got the whole world in His hands.

4. He's got the wind and the rain in his hands He's got the whole world in his hands.

Notice that the song "He's Got the Whole World in His Hands" has four strokes to the measure, so you would count 1 - 2 - 3 - 4 as you play C - / - / - / in the first full measure.

Try these practice songs, using the same chords. By listening carefully you can decide when to change chords: "Go Tell Aunt Rhody" (p. 77), "Clementine" (p. 40), "Skip to My Lou" (p. 67), "Did You Ever See A Lassie," "The More We Get Together" (p. 61), and "Goodbye, My Lover, Goodbye."

FINGERING

There are no set rules for Autoharp fingering. It is a matter of convenience and dexterity. Some players use one or two fingers, hopping from chord to chord. Others add the thumb or the little finger, a good combination on songs where the chords are far apart and a fast chord change is necessary.

However, for the majority of simple tunes, most people use the *index, middle,* and *ring* finger as in Fig. 12, placing them on the three principal chords in a particular chord grouping. As you can see, the index finger is on the C, the middle finger is on the G7, and the ring finger is on the F. These are the three principal chords in the key of C (A further discussion of chord groupings on the Autoharp is on page 163).

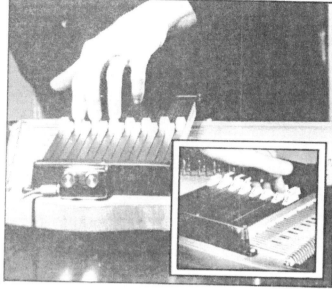

Fig. 12

The Autoharp shown above is equipped with a self-installed electronic pickup.

You are now ready to play a three chord song in the key of C Major.

MICHAEL, ROW THE BOAT ASHORE

Key of C
C, F, & G7

Chords used: C, F, G7, (Dm), & (Em)

1. Mi-chael row the boat a - shore. Hal - le - lu - Jah! Mi-chael

row the boat a - shore, Hal - le - lu - - Jah!

2. Sister help me trim the sail,
Hallelujah!
Sister help me trim the sail,
Hallelujah!

3. Jordan river is chilly and cold,
Hallelujah!
Chills the body but not the soul.
Hallelujah!

4. Land of Canaan on the other side,
Hallelujah!
Land of Canaan on the other side,
Hallelujah!

5. We are bound for the promised land,
Hallelujah!
We are bound for the promised land,
Hallelujah!

6. I have heard the good news too
Hallelujah!
I have heard the good news too
Hallelujah!

*A more advanced arrangement of this melody uses the Em and Dm chords.

If you have a 21 or 27 chord model and wish to experiment, use the chords in parenthesis beside the traditional chords. *Chords in parenthesis are always optional.* If you do not wish to use them continue stroking the previous one.

Notice that keeping your fingers in place over the three chord bars make it much easier to change chords quickly and smoothly.

If you play a 21 chord Autoharp and use the standard chord arrangement**, your fingers will fall naturally on the chord groupings. You still use the index, middle, and ring fingers. These fingers almost always form the points of a triangle (see Fig. 13 and 14). Notice that the 7th chords are placed so that they will be near the major and minor keys they have in common.

Some additional practice songs using three chords are: "The Man On The Flying Trapeze," "Little Brown Church in the Vale," "The Marine's Hymn," "The Happy Wanderer," "My Home's In Montana," Li'l Liza Jane," "Aloha Oe," "Silent Night," and "This Land Is Your Land."

**For diagrams of alternate chord arrangements see p. 163.

Using the fingering pictured in Fig. 12 and 13 (depending on the model you own) play the next song. It uses the three principal chords in the key of A minor.

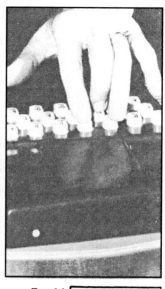

Fig. 13   Fig. 14

| Key of Am |
| Am, Dm, & E7 |

JOSHUA FIT THE BATTLE OF JERICHO

Chords used: Am, Dm, E7

Chorus:
Josh-ua fit the Bat-tle of___ Je-ri-cho, Je-ri-cho, Je-ri-cho___ Josh-ua fit the Bat-tle of___ Je-ri-cho and the walls came tum-bl-in' down.... Verse: You may talk a-bout your kings of Gi-de-on; You may talk a-bout your men of Saul, But there's none like good old Joshu-a At the Bat-tle of Jer-i-cho.

2. Well the Lord done told old Joshua,
   "You must do just what I say,
   March 'round that city seven times
   And the walls will tumble away."
Chorus: Joshua fit the Battle of Jericho, etc.

3. So up the walls of Jericho
   He marched with spear in hand,
   "Go blow them ram horns!" Joshua cried,
   'Cause the battle am in my hand!"
Chorus: Joshua fit the Battle of Jericho, etc.

LESSON 3: SIMPLE STRUMS

As you played the last two songs, many of you probably varied the strokes to make it more interesting, and in so doing made a rhythmic pattern of your own. You were playing in different *octaves*, or sections of the Autoharp.

Here are the three octaves as shown on the scale label below...

and the symbols used to indicate them...

$\oint$ = A STROKE IN THE LOWER OCTAVE

$\oint$ = A STROKE IN THE MIDDLE OCTAVE

$\oint$ = A STROKE IN THE HIGHER OCTAVE

$\uparrow$ = An UPSTROKE, played from the lower (bass) to the higher (treble) strings. If the Autoharp is on a table, the stroke would be away from your body.

$\downarrow$ = A DOWNSTROKE, played from the higher to the lower strings, toward your body.

If there are no octave designations on the strum patterns, the stroke may be in the octave of the player's choice.

For those of you who play the guitar or banjo, do not confuse "up" and "down"-strokes. What Autoharp players call an upstroke is to a guitar player a downstroke. Just think of the "up" as going to the higher strings, and the "down" as going toward the lower strings.

> **Definition:** When two or more of these strokes are combined in a rhythmic pattern you have a strum. A *strum*, then, is a *series of up or downstrokes played within one or more octaves (sections) of the Autoharp by one or more fingers in a rhythmic pattern.*

These sections are approximate areas only. You need not stroke the entire octave, nor be rigid about the number of strings sounded. There should be flexibilty and individuality in the playing of these patterns.

Use your thumb (with pick) to play this first strum, which combines an upstroke in the lower and an upstroke in the higher octave. In Autoharp notation it looks like this:

$$\uparrow \quad \uparrow \quad \uparrow \quad \uparrow$$

Combined with counting and traditional notation[**] it looks like this: (See Footnote, p. 19).

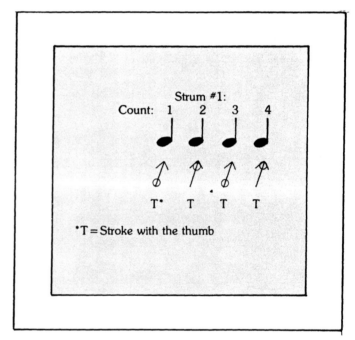

Now play Red River Valley using this strum. The pattern will only be shown over the first few bars, but should be played throughout the song. Notice that you use the three principal chords in the key of C, with a C7 added for richness.

RED RIVER VALLEY

Chords used: C, F, G7, & C7

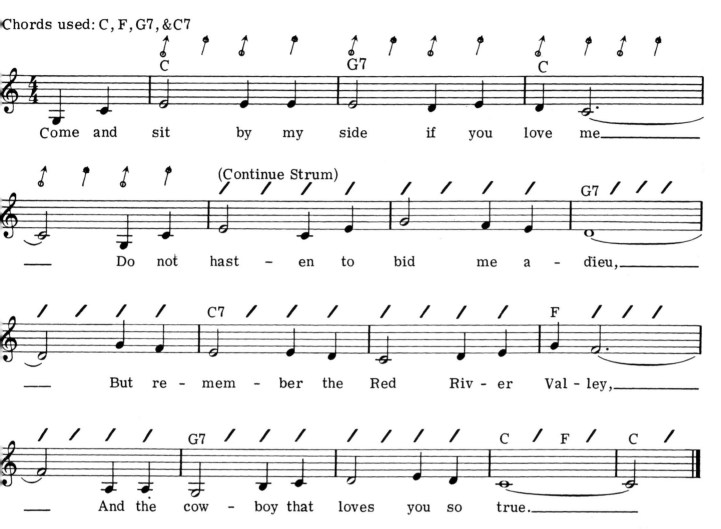

Come and sit by my side if you love me____
____ Do not hast – en to bid me a – dieu,____
____ But re – mem – ber the Red Riv – er Val – ley,____
____ And the cow – boy that loves you so true.____

Try a variation of this pattern, using a longer, brush-like stroke in the middle octave on counts of 2 and 4, and a heavier, shorter, accented stroke in the lower octave on counts 1 and 3.

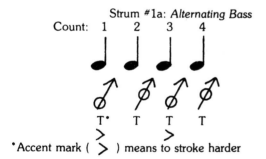

Strum #1a: *Alternating Bass*
Count: 1 2 3 4

*Accent mark (>) means to stroke harder

On the count of "1", stroke the very lowest string. On the count of "3" start the stroke several strings higher. You are still in the lower octave. If this strum were done on a guitar you would be hitting the two lower strings alternately. On the Autoharp you hit one or two strings at a time in different sections of the octave.

The notes in the preceding songs fall into groups of four. This is called 4/4 (four-quarter) time.

**It is not necessary to understand music notation to play these strums. Just count out loud where indicated and follow the strum symbols. Notation is included for those who use the Autoharp to teach music, and as an aid to better understanding the rhythmic pattern. On p. 7 there is an explanation of notation, timing and note values.

The next song falls into a pattern of three counts to a measure. This is called 3/4 (three-quarter) time. The strum pattern is a typical "oom-pah-pah" waltz rhythm with one upstroke in the lower octave followed by two in the higher octave. It looks like this: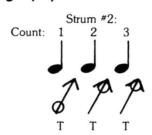

Strum #2:
Count: 1 2 3

Notice, also that you are playing in a new key—G Major. Locate the three principal chords: G, C, & D7.

Key of G
G, C, D7

Remember, the strum pattern is shown only on the first few bars, but played throughout the piece.

ON TOP OF OLD SMOKY

Chords used: G, C, &D7

On top of old smo - ky_____ All cov - ered with snow,_____ I lost my true lov - er_____ Came a court - in' too slow.

2. A-court-in's a pleasure,
   and parting's a grief,
   but a false-hearted lover
   is worse than a thief

3. A thief he may rob you,
   and tell you more lies
   than the ties on the railroad
   or the stars in the skies.

Try this variation with another 3/4 time song, using an upstroke in each of the three octaves:

Strum #2a:

Count: 1 2 3

T T T

THE STREETS OF LAREDO
(Cowboy's Lament)

Western Song

Chords used: C, F, G7, Am, &Dm

(Continue Strum)

As I_____ walked out in the streets of La - re do As I walked out in La - re do one day I saw a young cow-boy all draped in white lin - en, All draped in white lin - en as cold as the clay

20

'Since "The Streets of Laredo" is a slow, melancholy piece it also lends itself to this pattern: 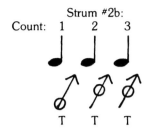 Make the first beat a short stroke in the lower octave, and the second and third beats longer brushes covering the entire middle octave.

Try these practice songs in 3/4 time: "Blow The Man Down," "Scarborough Fair," (p.124) "Happy Birthday To You," and "Amazing Grace". (p. 120)

LONESOME ROAD

Chords used: D, G, A7, D7, & Gm

Look down, look down that lone-some road, Hang down your head and sigh. The

Best of friends must part some day,— And why not you and I?

Other songs which lend themselves to this pattern are: "Old Folks At Home" (p. 53), "Foggy, Foggy Dew", (p.129) and "This Old Man" (p. 35).

Now, speed up the previous strum and add a downstroke on the second half of the 4th beat. It is a short stroke played in the middle octave with the thumb and a rotating wrist. The complete strum looks like this: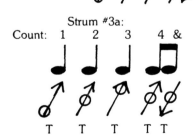

Be sure to play the last two strokes twice as fast as each of the other three.

LESSON 4: COMBINING UP AND DOWNSTROKES; Use of thumb and index finger.

Add a 4th beat to strum #2a and you have this 4/4 pattern:

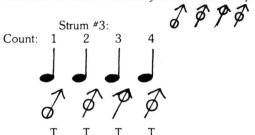

Play this pattern slowly several times. To help you remember it, repeat the octave names as you practice: lower-middle-higher-middle; lower-middle-higher-middle, etc. Then look at the next song and locate the principal chords in the key of D major: D, G, & A7.

> Key of D
> D, G, & A7

Gm and D7 are added to enrich the harmony (Those with diminished chords on their Autoharp can use a C# dim. in place of the Gm). Notice, also, that in several measures you must change chords in the middle of the strum pattern.

Get the strum going and see how much more interesting it becomes as the tempo (speed) increases. The strokes also become shorter and lighter. This pattern can be played on the previous song, using two patterns in each measure.

A slight variation *introduces the index finger* on the final down-stroke. A finger pick can be used (See Fig. 8, p. 13).

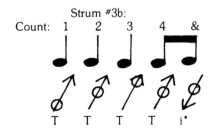

*i = Stroke with the index finger

21

Keep the strum light and fast and try it on this old favorite.

POLLY WOLLY DOODLE

Chords used: D&A7

Oh I went down south for to see my Sal, singing
Pol-ly wol-ly doo-dle all the day My__ Sal she is a__
spunk - y gal, Sing-ing Pol - ly wol - ly doo - dle all the
day. Fare thee well, fare thee well, Fare thee
well my fair - y fey, For I'm goin' to Lou'-si- an - a for to
see my Su - si- an - na, Sing-ing Pol - ly wol - ly doo-dle all the day.

2. Oh, a grasshopper sitting on a railroad track,
Singing polly-wolly-doodle all the day,
A picking his teeth with a carpet tack,
Sing polly-wolly doodle all the day.
Fare the well, etc.

Here is another excellent song with a minor sound, which lends itself to this strum. Musicians will recognize the harmony as being in the Dorian mode. This is an old scale form using no key signature. If you have a dulcimer player handy, this would make a fine duet.

DRUNKEN SAILOR

Chords used: Dm, C, & F

What shall we do with the Drunk-en Sail-or, What shall we do with the Drunk-en Sail-or,

(Continue Strum)

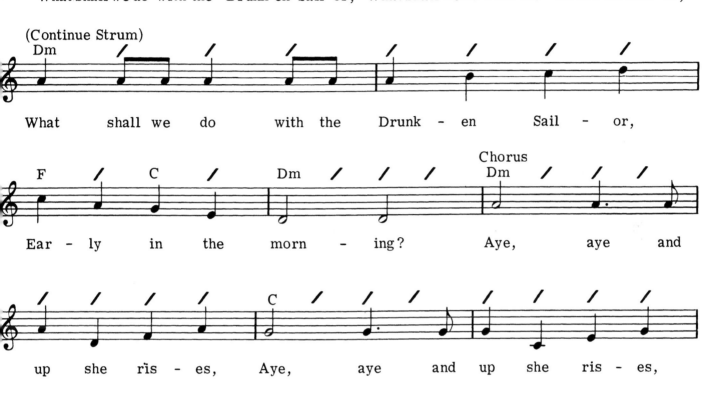

What shall we do with the Drunk - en Sail - or,

Chorus

Ear - ly in the morn - ing? Aye, aye and

up she ris - es, Aye, aye and up she ris - es,

Aye, aye and up she ris - es, Ear - ly in the morn - ing.

Folk songs such as "Buffalo Gals," "Swanee River," (p. 53), and "Little Brown Jug," (p. 64) also sound great with this pattern.

They can be played using the three principal chords in the major keys learned so far: C, G, or D.

LESSON 5: THE ARPEGGIANDO STROKE
(pronounced: ar-peg-ee-an-doe)

Definition: This is a gentle stroke played slowly up and down over two or more octaves of the Autoharp.

The upstroke (away from the body) is accomplished like this:

The downstroke (toward the body) is accomplished like this:

Fig. 16

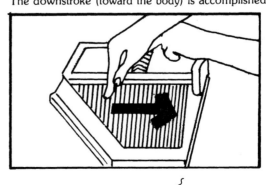

Fig. 17

The sign for an upstroke is: ↗

The sign for a downstroke is: ↙

Press the thumb and index finger together, slipping the index finger forward as you approach the highest strings, ready for a smooth transition to the downstroke. Thus, it is the fleshy part of the thumb which touches the strings on the upstroke and the fleshy part of the index finger on the downstroke.

When the two strokes are combined in one graceful motion, a flowing, harp-like sound is produced. The sign for this combined up and downstroke is:

A felt pick can be used, but it is more beautiful and controlled if done only with the finger and thumb (without picks). Since this is a free-flowing type of sound, it is not important how many measures are covered by each stroke. Play the way it sounds and feels best to you. There will probably be one to two measures for each combined up and downstroke.

HUSH, LITTLE BABY

Chords used: G&D7

Hush lit-tle ba - by, don't say a word, Pa-pa's gon-na buy you a mock-ing bird, And

(Continue Strum)

if that mock - ing bird don't sing, Pa-pa's gon-na buy you a dia - mond ring.

2. And if that diamond ring is brass,
   Papa's gonna buy you a lookin-glass,
   And if that looking-glass gets broke,
   Papa's gonna buy you a billy goat.

3. And if that billy goat don't pull,
   Papa's gonna buy you a cart and bull.
   And if that cart and bull turn over,
   Papa's gonna buy you a dog named Rover.

4. And if that dog named Rover don't bark,
   Papa's gonna buy you a horse and cart.
   And if that horse and cart fall down,
   You'll still be the sweetest little baby in town.

For those whose fingers have not yet acquired callouses, try playing the second verse, using the fingernail of the index finger on the upstroke and the fingernail of the thumb on the downstroke. The fingers are still touching, but the index finger, instead of the thumb, leads the way.

Many old songs like "Down In The Valley" (p. 38), "Kum Ba Yah" (p. 48), "Foggy, Foggy Dew" (p.129) lend themselves well to the arpeggiando stroke. Practice them at this time, listening for the chord changes.

The arpeggiando stroke can be combined with strokes in other octaves to make simple as well as complex strum patterns. This next one combines an upstroke in the lower octave with two upward arpeggiandos, starting in the middle octave. A thumb pick may be used until the thumb is toughened up, or the arpeggiando stroke can be done with the fingernail of the index finger.

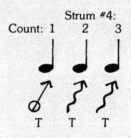

Again, watch for new chords and changes in the middle of the strum in the last three measures.

24

COCKLES AND MUSSELS

Chords used: C, F, G7, Am, Dm, A7, &D7

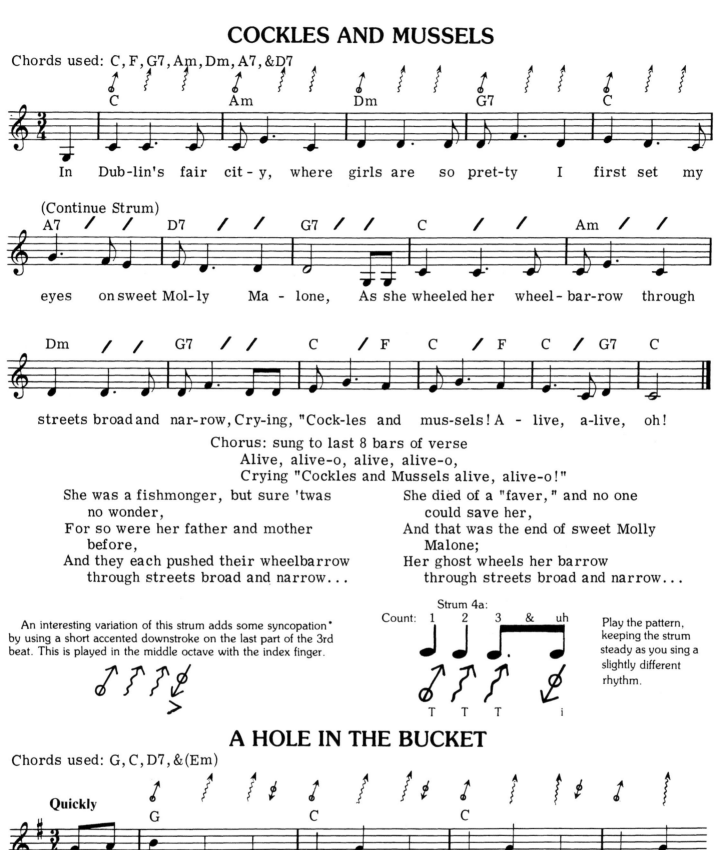

In Dub-lin's fair cit-y, where girls are so pret-ty I first set my

(Continue Strum)

A7 / / D7 / / G7 / / C / / Am / /

eyes on sweet Mol-ly Ma - lone, As she wheeled her wheel-bar-row through

Dm / / G7 / / C / F C / F C / G7 C

streets broad and nar-row, Cry-ing, "Cock-les and mus-sels! A - live, a-live, oh!

Chorus: sung to last 8 bars of verse
Alive, alive-o, alive, alive-o,
Crying "Cockles and Mussels alive, alive-o!"

She was a fishmonger, but sure 'twas
no wonder,
For so were her father and mother
before,
And they each pushed their wheelbarrow
through streets broad and narrow...

She died of a "faver," and no one
could save her,
And that was the end of sweet Molly
Malone;
Her ghost wheels her barrow
through streets broad and narrow...

An interesting variation of this strum adds some syncopation*
by using a short accented downstroke on the last part of the 3rd
beat. This is played in the middle octave with the index finger.

Strum 4a:

Count: 1   2   3   &   uh

Play the pattern,
keeping the strum
steady as you sing a
slightly different
rhythm.

T   T   T   i

A HOLE IN THE BUCKET

Chords used: G, C, D7, &(Em)

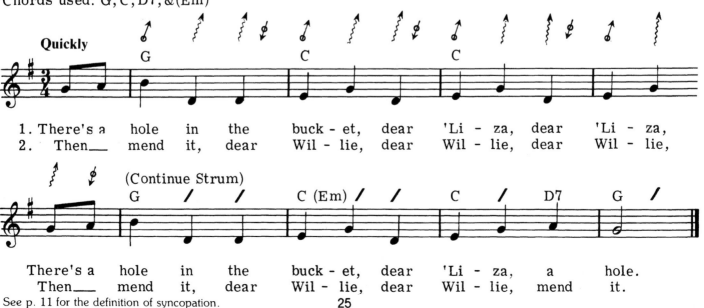

Quickly

G   C   C

1. There's a hole in the buck - et, dear 'Li - za, dear 'Li - za,
2. Then__ mend it, dear Wil - lie, dear Wil - lie, dear Wil - lie,

(Continue Strum)

G / / C (Em) / / C / D7 G /

There's a hole in the buck - et, dear 'Li - za, a hole.
Then__ mend it, dear Wil - lie, dear Wil - lie, mend it.

See p. 11 for the definition of syncopation.   25

Here is another simple strum which can be used on this old blues melody.

WAYFARING STRANGER

Chords used: Am, Dm, F, & C

I just a poor___ way-far-in' stran-ger___

___ a trav'-lin' through___ this world of woe___

___ But there's no sick - - ness, toil or troub-le___

___ to that bright land___ to which I go.

I'm go-ing home___ to see my moth-er,___

___ I'm go-ing there___ no more to roam,___

___ I'm just a go - - ing o-ver Jor-dan,___

___ I'm just a go - ing o-ver home.___

* Note the beautiful dissonance between the voice and the Dm Chord. This adds to the sad feeling of the song.

26

A variation of the previous strum uses four strokes to the measure.

Count: 1   2   3   4

T   T   T   T

SHENANDOAH

Chords used: C, F, G7, Am, & (Em)

Slowly

C

F

1. Oh, Shen-an-doah,___ I long to hear you, A - way,_____ you roll-ing

C

(Continue Strum)

Am   (Em) F

riv - er.___ Oh Shen-an - doah___ I long to hear you, A -

C   /   Am   /   C (Em) / / /   D7 / / /   G7   C   /

way,_____ we're bound a - way, 'Cross the wide Mis - sou - ri.

2. The white man loved the Indian maiden,
   Away, you rolling river
   With notions his canoe was laden,
   Away, we're bound away,
   'Cross the wide Missouri.

3. O, Shenandoah, I love your daughter,
   Away, you rolling river
   I'll take her 'cross the rolling water,
   Away, we're bound away,
   'Cross the wide Missouri.

4. O, Shenandoah, I'm bound to leave you,
   Away, you rolling river,
   O, Shenandoah, I'll not deceive you,
   Away, we're bound away,
   'Cross the wide Missouri.

This pattern also fits beautifully on such songs as "Swing Low, Sweet Chariot," "Long, Long Ago" (p. 45), and "Black Is The Color Of My True Love's Hair" (p. 122)

LESSON 6: The "CHURCH LICK"

This is an adaptation of a guitar style made famous by Woody Guthrie. It is done with an alternating bass stroke played by the thumb in the lower octave, followed by a *rapid* up and down arpeggiando using the loose fist (LF). Figure 18 shows the hand position for a loose fist. The hand is relaxed as the fingernails brush across the strings. When you become proficient doing this strum there will be a spontaneous "fanning out" of the entire hand just before the downstroke arpeggiando is performed. This is shown from the front view in Figure 23. No picks are worn on the fingers as the entire hand lifts off and hits the strings with a fast, glancing stroke. This strum can also be played with a flat plastic pick as in Fig. 19.

Remember, the arpeggiando stroke covers at least two octaves.

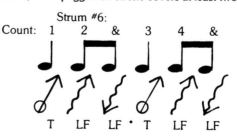

Strum #6:

Count: 1   2   &   3   4   &

T   LF   LF • T   LF   LF

•LF = Loose Fist

27

You have already played an alternating bass in strum #1a, but this time start the thumb (bass) stroke on a higher section of the lower octave on the 1st beat, moving to a lower section of the octave on the 3rd beat. This is the opposite of the bass pattern in strum #1a. Either way is correct, but it's always fun to experiment. No two strokes are exactly alike.

Play strum #6 on this traditional folk tune.

Fig. 18 Playing with the Loose Fist Fig. 19 Playing with the flat pick

CINDY

(21 and 27 chord model)

Chords used: D, G, A7,

1. Oh have you seen my Cin - dy, She comes from 'way down
2. I wish I was an ap - ple A - hang - in' in a

(Continue Strum)

south, And she's so sweet the hon - ey bees just
tree, And ev' - ry time my sweet-heart passed she'd

swarm a - round her mouth CHORUS: Get a - long home, Cin - dy
take a bite of me.

Cin - dy, Get a - long home, Cin - dy Cin - dy, Get a - long

home, Cin - dy Cin - dy, I'll mar - ry you some day.

Additional practice songs for this pattern are: "I'm On My Way," "The Saints," (p. 106), and "Redwing."

3. I wish I had a needle,
As fine as I could sew;
I'd sew the girls to my coattail,
And down the road I'd go...
Chorus: Get along, etc.

HOLDING THE AUTOHARP APPALACHIAN STYLE

Fig. 20 Holding without strap.

Fig. 21 With strap attached.

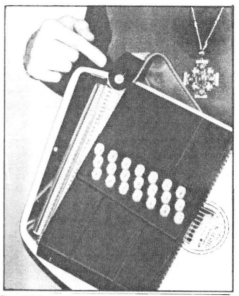

Fig. 22 Instrument with strap fittings.

Now, try this variation of strum #6.

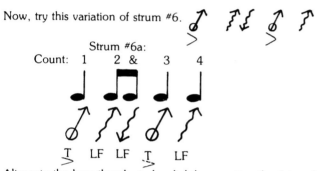

Alternate the bass thumb stroke slightly accenting the 1st and 3rd beats.

Hold your Autoharp in your arms Appalachian style, as in Fig. 20. Notice how much freer your right arm is to move back and forth across all three octaves. Once you get used to holding the instrument this way you'll find that the faster, more advanced strums can be played with greater accuracy and speed, since there is no more "crossing over" of the hands. The fingering, of course, will be different. It is up to the player to choose the finger patterns which suit him or her best.

As you play this pattern on the following old gospel hymn, notice how your fingers almost automatically fan out from the Loose Fist position. It becomes less of a wrist than a hand motion as the strum gets faster.

Play two strum patterns per measure.

Fig. 23 Loose fist during "Church Lick."

DO, LORD

(21 and 27 chord model)

Chords used: G, C, D7, G7, Em, & B7

Rousingly

G ... G7

I've got a home in glo - ry - land that out - shines the sun.

(Continue Strum)

C ... G

I've got a home in glo - ry - land that out - shines the sun.

G ... D7 B7 ... Em

I've got a home in glo - ry - land that out - shines the sun___

G ... D7 ... G

'way be - yond___ the blue.   Do, Lord   O do, Lord,   O

... G7 C

do re - mem - ber me,   Do, Lord   O do, Lord   O
(O Lordy)

... G ... D7

do re - mem - ber me,   Do, Lord   O do, Lord,   O
(Hallelujah)

B7 ... Em ... G ... D7 ... G C G

do re - mem - ber me_____   'way be - yond___ the blue.

30

For those who wish to try a more advanced strum combining the thumb, index finger, and arpeggiando stroke, practice the following:

When played fast, it sounds like "Boom - chicka - boom - chick." If you repeat the phrase it will help you learn the rhythm. The thumb quickly follows the first arpeggiando stroke, almost as if it were a continuation of the Loose Fist (LF). This is a forerunner of many advanced strums. The chords change in the middle of each pattern, but the beat must be kept steady over the contrasting rhythm of the piece.

Since this next song is written in 2/4 time with only two beats to the measure, Strum #7 could be counted as follows:

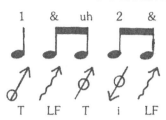

This is the identical finger pattern; only the musical notation is different.

THE CALTON WEAVER

Chords used: C, F, G7, Am, Dm, & (Em)

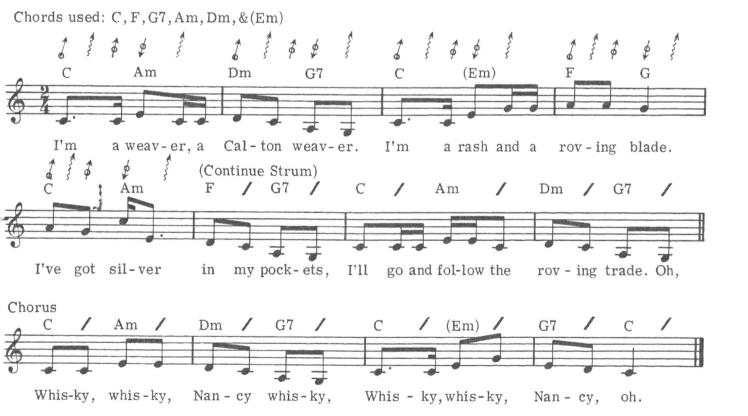

I'm a weav-er, a Cal-ton weav-er. I'm a rash and a rov-ing blade.

(Continue Strum)

I've got sil-ver in my pock-ets, I'll go and fol-low the rov-ing trade. Oh,

Chorus

Whis-ky, whis-ky, Nan-cy whis-ky, Whis-ky, whis-ky, Nan-cy, oh.

Fast country songs lend themselves to these last three patterns.
Try them on "Sourwood Mountain" (p. 79), "Crawdad Song" (p 139), "Oh, Susanna" (p. 78), and "Jesse James".

LESSON 7: MOUNTAIN STRUMS

There are hundreds of strum patterns which have been developed out of the picking styles of country, folk, and bluegrass musicians. Those who have listened to Ernest V. "Pop" Stoneman, Kilby Snow, Mike Seeger, and the late Mother Maybelle Carter know the Appalachian Mountain sound most closely associated with the Autoharp. The following 15 patterns will show you a variety of ways to play this sound. Try them all. Choose the ones best suited to you and practice them slowly, building up speed and accuracy. The more advanced mountain strums are found in the sections on banjo rolls (p.142) and bluegrass melody picking (p.75)*, combining both melody and rhythmic patterns in an exciting, intricate way.

THUMB — BRUSH

To build up skill in country picking, start with a short, accented stroke with the thumb in the lower octave, followed by a longer stroke covering the entire middle octave. This brush stroke is actually a continuation of the thumb stroke. It starts where the thumb stops and the thumb never leaves the strings. Wear a thumb pick if you wish.

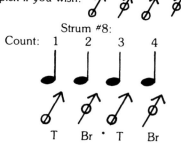

Strum #8:

Count: 1   2   3   4

T   Br   T   Br

*Br = Brush with the thumb

After you have practiced this you will notice that as the tempo increases your thumb automatically starts to brush the strings in a downstroke on the 2nd half of the 2nd beat. This leads into the next pattern, which combines a stroke in the lower octave followed by a fast up and down—brush in the middle octave. Be sure the wrist is flexible and rotates, as with all fast strumming. Again, the entire strum is done with the thumb, which never leaves the strings.

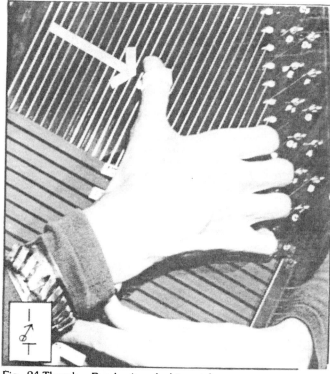

Fig. 24 Thumb—Brush, Appalachian style

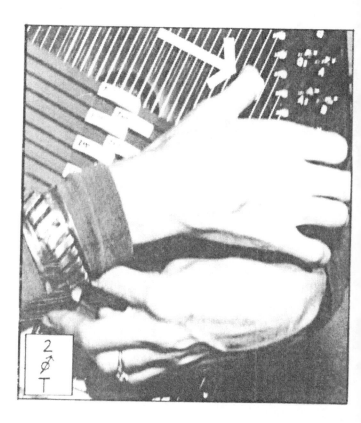

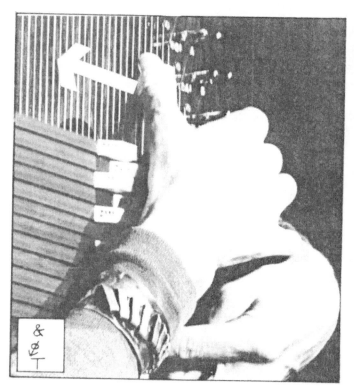

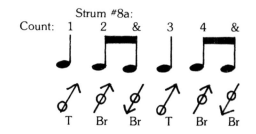

Strum #8a:

Count: 1   2   &   3   4   &

T   Br   Br   T   Br   Br

Try both variations with the next song.

*See "Country Pickin' On The Autoharp," Meg Peterson, Mel Bay Publications, Inc., Pacific, Mo. 63069, to be published 1980.

DOWN BY THE RIVERSIDE
(Ain't Gonna Study War No More)

Chords used: G, C, D7, & G7

Gon-na lay down my sword and shield Down by the
riv-er - side, Down by the riv-er - side, Down by the
riv-er - side, Gon-na lay down my sword and shield Down by the
riv-er - side, And stud-y_____ war no more._____ I ain't gon-na

Chorus

stud-y____ war no more, I ain't gon-na stud-y____ war no
more, I ain't gon-na stud-y_____ war no more._____
____ I ain't gon-na stud - y war no more, I ain't gon-na stud - y war no
more, I ain't gon-na stud - y_____ war no more._____

I'm gonna join hands with everyone,
Down by the riverside, down by the riverside,
Down by the riverside.
I'm gonna join hands with everyone,
Down by the riverside,
And study war no more.

I'm gonna put on my long white robe...

I'm gonna talk with the Prince of peace...

33

Other songs using the same chords and strum pattern are "Mountain Dew", "Hard and It's Hard", and "When The Saints Go Marching In" (p.106). Many country rock hits employ this rhythm as well.

In the next strum the pattern and timing are the same, but a loose fist (LF) is used instead of the thumb for the fast up and down-strokes in the middle octave. This is similar to the "Church Lick", but the strokes are faster and confined to the middle octave. In both these patterns an alternating bass adds interest, but requires a lot of concentration when the patterns are new (See Fig. 18 for position of Loose Fist).

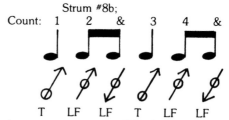

Since this next song is in a fast 2/4 rhythm you can also count: "1-and-uh, 2-and-uh," using the rhythm of Strum #8C.

DIXIE

Chords used: C, F, G7, D7, & C7

34

LESSON 8: THE "CARTER LICK"

 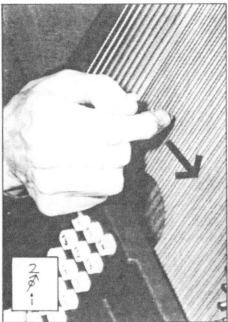 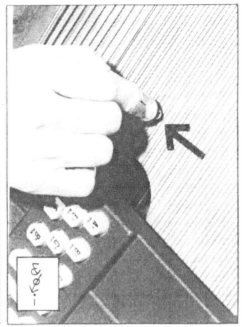

Fig. 25: "Carter Lick"

This is also called "Scratch Style," an adaptation of the guitar style made famous by the Carter Family. As in the previous strum, it uses an upstroke with the thumb in the lower octave, but the rapid up and down strokes in the middle octave ↗↘ are played by the fingernail of the index finger of the right hand with or without a pick.

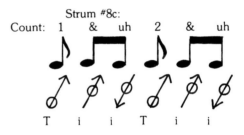

After you have mastered this pattern try it on the next song. You will notice that it is in 2/4 time with only two beats to the measure. Therefore, the count it:

"1 and-uh, 2 and-uh"

THIS OLD MAN

Chords used: D, G, & A7

This old man,   he played "one",   He played "Nick-nack" on   my drum, With a

Chorus (Continue Strum)

"Nick-nack pad-dy whack, give my dog a bone."   This old man came roll-ing home.

...two, He played "nick-nack" on my shoe.   ...six, He played "nick-nack" on my sticks.
...three, He played "nick-nack" on my knee.   ...seven, He played "nick-nack" up to heaven.
...four, He played "nick-nack" on my door.   ...eight, He played "nick-nack" on my plate.
...five, He played "nick-nack" on my hive.   ...nine, He played "nick-nack" on my spine.
...ten, He played "nick-nack" once again.

This next strum *introduces the middle finger*, which plays a downstroke in the higher octave. *Keep the same count as before.* To execute this pattern rapidly the index and middle fingers will barely touch two or three strings.

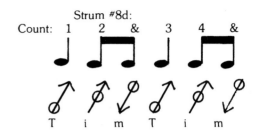

Strum #8d:

Count: 1 2 & 3 4 &

T i m T i m

m = Stroke with the middle finger

 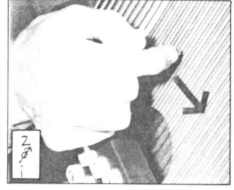 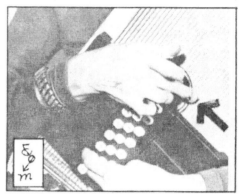

Fig. 26: Mountain Strum #8d:

JIMMY CRACK CORN

Chords used: D, G & A7

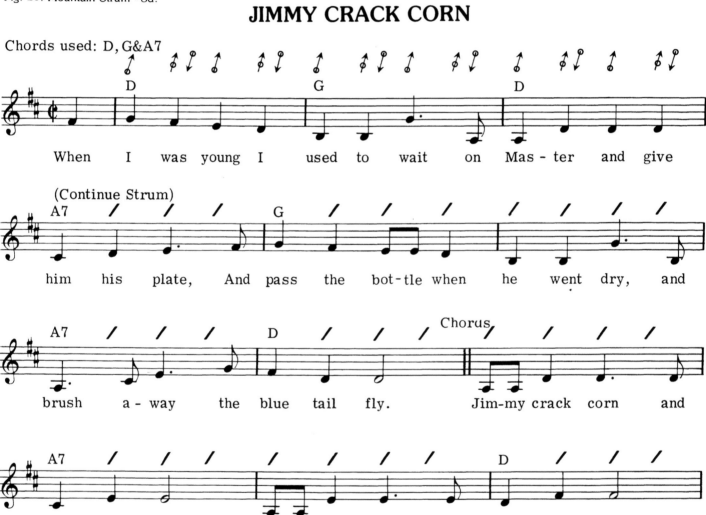

When I was young I used to wait on Mas - ter and give

(Continue Strum)

him his plate, And pass the bot-tle when he went dry, and

brush a - way the blue tail fly. Jim-my crack corn and

I don't care, Jim-my crack corn and I don't care,

Jim-my crack corn and I don't care, my Mas-ter's gone a - way.

36

The next strum is a prelude to *double thumbing*, a banjo technique discussd on p 102. It calls for some fast work with the thumb as it moves back and forth between the lower and middle octaves.

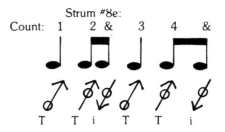

The next song is written in the key of F major. The principal chords are: F, Bb, & C7.

WABASH CANNONBALL

Key of F
F, Bb & C7

Chords used: F, Bb, C7, F7, & C

From the great At - lan - tic O - cean to the great Pa - cif - ic shore, from the queen of flow - ing ri - vers to the south - land by the shore. She's might - y tall and hand - some and quite well known by all. She's the com - bi - na - tion of the Wa - bash Can - non - ball.

There are many more songs suitable for these mountain strums, such as "Yellow Rose of Texas" (p. 73), "Bile 'Dem Cabbage Down", "There Is A Tavern In The Town", and "Camptown Races" (p. 45). Practice them, using the three principal chords in the key of C, G, D, or F. The key you choose, of course, will depend on your singing range.

The timing for the five previous strums has remained the same; only the fingering has changed. Now we move from 4/4 time to 3/4 time for the next two patterns.

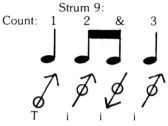

LESSON 9: SCRATCH STYLE IN 3/4 TIME

You can see that this is similar to Strum #8c in the use of the thumb and index finger. To get started, play this slow country ballad.

DOWN IN THE VALLEY

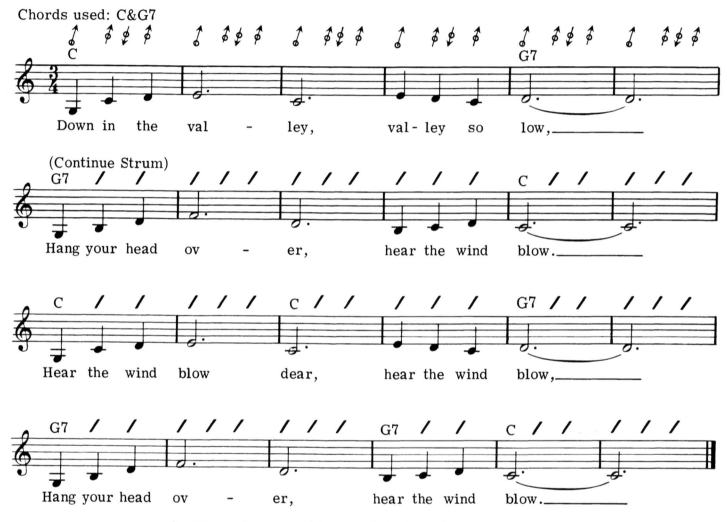

Chords used: C&G7

Down in the val - ley, val - ley so low,_____

(Continue Strum)

Hang your head ov - er, hear the wind blow._____

Hear the wind blow dear, hear the wind blow,_____

Hang your head ov - er, hear the wind blow._____

2. Roses love sunshine, violets love dew;
Angels in heaven know I love you.
Know I love you, dear, Know I love you.
Angels in heaven know I love you.

DOUBLE FINGER SCRATCH

To add volume and control to your scratch style, use the fingernails of both the index and middle fingers of the right hand to play the scratch. To vary the pattern, add an extra stroke on the final half of the 3rd beat.

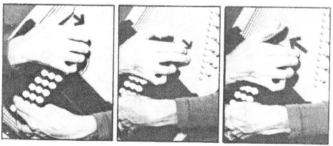

Fig. 27: Double Finger Scratch

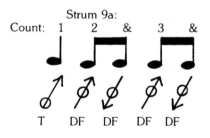

DF = Simultaneous scratch stroke with two fingers (index and middle)

MY BONNIE

Chords used: G, C, &D7

G   C   G

My Bon-nie lies o-ver the o-cean,_____ My

(Continue Strum)   D7

Bon-nie lies o-ver the sea._____ My

G   C   G   C

Bon-nie lies o-ver the o-cean,_____ O bring back my

D7   G

Bon-nie to me._____

Chorus:

G   C

Bring   back,   bring   back,   Oh,

D7   G

Bring back my Bon-nie to me,   to me;

C

Bring   back,   bring   back,   O

D7   G

bring back my Bon-nie to me._____

SIMPLE THREE FINGER PICKING

This next strum uses the same timing as the Double Finger Scratch, but is played in all three octaves by the thumb, middle, and index finger in turn.

Strum #10:

Count: 1   2   &   3   &

T   m   i   T   m

39

CLEMENTINE

Chords used: D&A7

D

In a cav - ern, In a can - yon, ex - ca - va - ting for a

A7 ... **D** (Continue Strum)

mine, Dwelt a min - er for - ty nin - er and his

A7 ... **D** ... Chorus:

daugh - ter clem-en - tine. Oh my dar - lin, oh my

... **A7**

dar - lin, oh my dar - lin Clem-en - tine, You are

... **D** ... **A7** ... **D**

lost and gone for - ev - er, dread-ful sor - ry, Clem-en - tine.

2. Light she was, and like a fairy, and her shoes were number nine,
   Herring boxes without topses, sandals were for Clementine. (Chorus)
3. Drove she ducklings to the water every morning just at nine,
   Hit her foot against a splinter, fell into the foaming brine. (Chorus)
4. Ruby lips above the water, blowing bubbles soft and fine,
   Sad for me! I was no swimmer, so I lost my Clementine. (Chorus)

SIMPLE ARPEGGIO STRUM

Another three finger strum is a forerunner of the more advanced Arpeggio strums (p.117).The player gently plucks as few strings as possible in the designated octave. As you can see by Fig. 28 the thumb moves up on the 3rd beat. It is a gentle, flowing pattern.

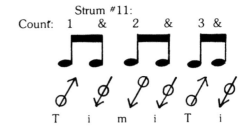

Strum #11:

Count: 1 & 2 & 3 &

T i m i T i

Fig. 28: Simple Arpeggio Strum

HOME ON THE RANGE

Chords used: G, C, D7, A7, G7, (Cm), &(Em)

Oh, give me a home where the buf - fa - lo roam where the deer and the an - tel - ope play;_____ Where sel - dom is heard a dis - cour - ag - ing word and the skies are not cloud - y all day._____

Chorus:

Home, home on the range,_____ where the deer and the an - tel - ope play;_____ Where sel - dom is heard a dis - cour - ag - ing word and the skies are not cloud - y all day._____

2. How often at night when the heavens are bright
   With the light from the glittering stars,
   Have I stood there amazed and asked as I gazed,
   If their glory exceeds that of ours.

(Chorus)

LESSON 10: INTRODUCTION TO TRAVIS PICKING

This is a type of three finger guitar picking which adapts itself well to the Autoharp. It derives its name from the guitar style of Merle Travis. The thumb alternates with the index and middle fingers of the right hand. The thumb plays an upstroke on each beat and the index and middle fingers alternate with a downstroke off the beat. *Each stroke is played in a slightly different section of the octave so the strum never becomes monotonous or heavy.*

What actually happens in this rapid pattern is that the thumb and fingers try to pick only one string at a time. This is done by keeping the stroke short so the fingers stop automatically at the first string that is sounded. The arrows merely indicate the direction of the picking motion.

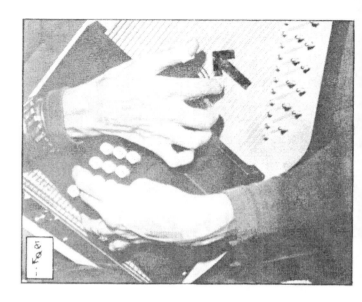

Fig. 29: Travis Picking in 3/4

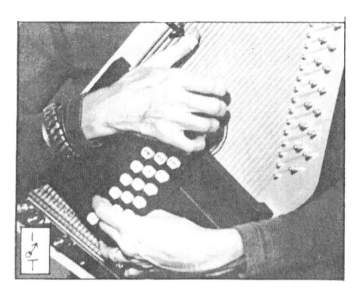

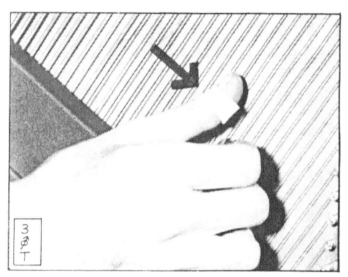

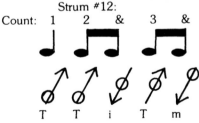

Strum #12:

Notice how the thumb moves gradually toward the higher strings. The 2nd beat, of course, is in a higher section of the octave, although it is written the same in the diagram.

SWEET BETSY FROM PIKE

Chords used: C, F, G7, G, Am, &(Em)

Did you ev – er hear tell of sweet Bet – sy from Pike, Who

crossed the wide prai – ries with her lov – er, Ike. With

two yoke of ox – en and one spot – ted hog, A___

tall Shang – hai roost – er, an old yel – low dog?

Chorus Sing___ too – ral – i, oo – ral – i, oo – ral – i ay, Sing___

too – ral – i, oo – ral – i, oo – ral – i ay.

One evening quite early they camped on the
    Platte,
'Twas near by the road on a green shady
    flat;
Where Betsy, quite tired, lay down to
    repose,
While with wonder Ike gazed on his Pike
    County rose.

They stopped at Salt Lake to inquire the
    way,
Where Brigham declared that sweet Betsy
    should stay.
But Betsy got frightened and ran like a
    deer,
While Brigham stood pawing the ground
    like a steer.

This same country pattern can also be used effectively on old favorites such as the next tune.

SIDEWALKS OF NEW YORK

(East Side, West Side)

Now that you've limbered up your fingers, add another down-stroke with the middle finger in the higher octave, and change the strum, slightly, to one of perpetual motion, moving from the higher to the lower strings. Keep the strokes light, and notice how well the pattern sounds on the two previous songs.

It has often been noted that Travis picking of this kind gives the effect of syncopation. That is because it has a steady thumb beat while the fingers fill in on the off-beat. It is actually a straight eighth note pattern.

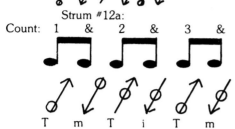

Now try the same two patterns in 4/4 time in the next lesson.

LESSON 11: TRAVIS PICKING IN 4/4 TIME

There is a natural curve to the following pattern, moving toward the higher, then back to the middle octave.

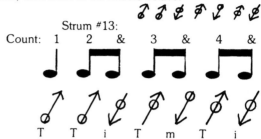

LONG, LONG AGO

Chords used: C&G7

Thomas H. Bayly

Tell me the tales that to me were so dear, Long, long a-go,

Long, long a-go, Sing me the song I de-light-ed to hear,

Long, long a-go, long a-go.

Now you are come, all my grief is re-moved.

Let me for-get that so long you have roved.

Let me be - lieve that you love as you loved.

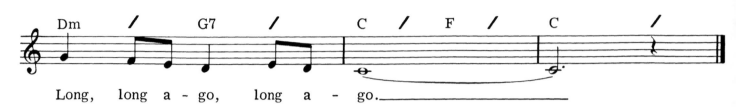

Long, long a - go, long a - go._____

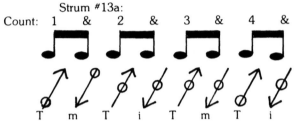

In the next strum, a stroke is added on the second half of the first beat. As in strum 12a, you jump immediately to the higher octave and work back to the lower.

Try this pattern on the following song. Since the strum is fast, use two complete patterns in each measure. This means that you will count to 8. To write the strum in exact notation would be confusing.

'TIS A GIFT TO BE SIMPLE

Chords used: F, B♭, C7, & G7

'Tis a gift to be sim-ple, 'tis a gift to be free, 'tis a

gift to come down where you ought to be, And

when we find our-selves in the place just right, 'Twill

be in the val-ley of love and de-light When true sim-

pli - ci - ty is gained, to bow and to bend we____

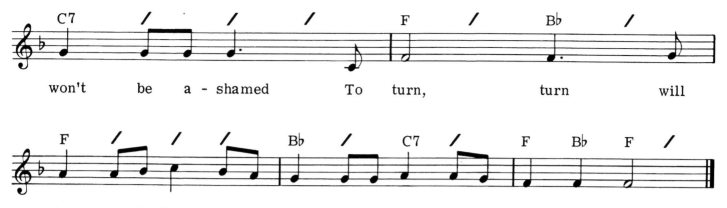

won't   be   a - shamed   To   turn,   turn   will

be   our de-light   'til   by   turn - ing and turn - ing   we   come   out   right.

Many modern pop, rock, and folk-rock songs sound great with these and other variations of three finger picking. Combined with melody (p.72) they are both challenging and pleasing to the ear!

LESSON 12: TRAVIS PICKING WITH THE PINCH

The pinch (P) adds a great deal of variety to all kinds of Autoharp picking. The next strum requires a wide pinch with the thumb and middle finger. The thumb plucks a string in the lower octave while the middle finger plucks one in the higher octave. As in the previous strums, the fingers move up and down the entire length of the strings.

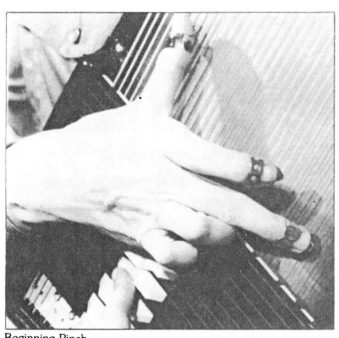

Beginning Pinch

Fig. 30

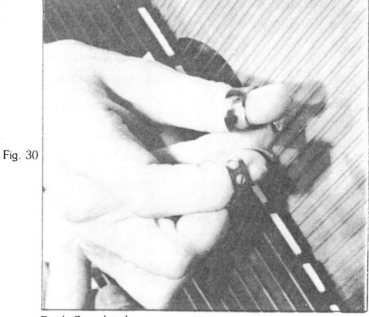

Pinch Completed

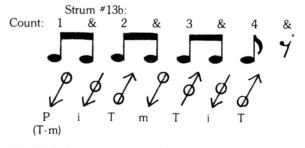

P = Pinch using the thumb and middle finger (T-m)

·⅞ = Eighth rest. Pause on this beat and get ready for the next Pinch.

47

On this next song, notice that you're playing a steady beat while the melody has a different rhythm. Get a friend to sing while you learn the pattern. Notice, also, how often the chords change in the middle of the strum.

KUM BA YAH
(Come By Here)

Chords used: D, G, A7, & (Em)

Kum-ba - ya, My Lord._____ Kum-ba - ya,_____ Kum-ba -

(Continue Strum)

ya, My Lord,_____ Kum-ba - ya._____ Kum-ba -

ya, My Lord,_____ Kum-ba - ya,_____ Oh,

Lord_____ Kum - ba - ya._____

2. Someone's crying Lord, Kum-ba-ya. (3 times)
   Oh, Lord, Kum-ba-ya

3. Someone's praying Lord, Kum-ba-ya. (3 times)
   Oh, Lord, Kum-ba-ya.

4. Someone's singing Lord, Kum-ba-ya. (3 times)
   Oh, Lord, Kum-ba-ya.

Here is another variation using the Pinch with Travis picking. The second half of the first beat is not played, but the final one is.

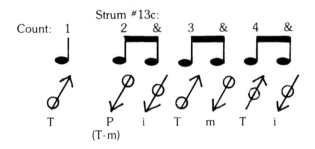

OH, DEM GOLDEN SLIPPERS

Chords used: G, C, D7 & Am

Oh, my gold - en slip-pers are— laid a - way, 'cause I don't 'spect to

(Continue strum)

wear them 'til my wed - ding day, And my long - tailed coat, that I

loved so well, I will wear up in the char-iot in the morn. And my

long white robe that I bought last June I'm— goin' to get changed 'cause it

fits too soon, And the old gray horse that I used to drive, I will

hitch him to the char-iot in the morn. Chorus Oh, dem gol - den slip-pers,

Oh, dem gol - den slip-pers, Gol - den slip-pers I'm— go-in' to wear Be -

cause they look so neat Oh, dem gol-den slip-pers, Oh, dem

gol-den slip-pers, gol-den slip-pers I'm go-in' to wear to walk the gol-den street.

A final mountain strum combines the scratch style (Carter Lick),

(p. 35) and Travis picking into one pattern:

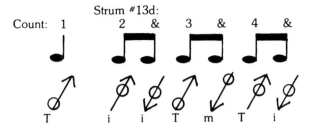

SHE'LL BE COMIN' 'ROUND THE MOUNTAIN
(When She Comes)

Chords used: G, C, D7, &G7

2. Oh, we'll all go out to meet her...
3. She'll be drivin' six white horses...
4. Oh, we'll kill the old red rooster...
5. And we'll all have chicken and dumplin's...

LESSON 13: MELODY STRUMMING

To understand the concept of melody on the Autoharp, play the following excerpt from "Swanee River." Stroke with the rhythm of the tune all the way across the strings as in Simple Strumming.

SWANEE RIVER
(Old Folks At Home)

Chords used: C, F, &G7

By Stephen Foster

'Way　　down up on the　Swa - nee　Riv-er,　　Far,　　far a - way.

There's　where my heart is　turn ing　ev-er,　There's where the old　folks　stay.

Notice how the chord changes are more frequent than in Simple Strumming. Now, play the song again and vary the stroke so you go up and down with the melody. You're no longer stroking all the strings, but modifying the length of your stroke to bring out the melody.

Next, press down the C chord and make short intermittent strokes with your thumb or index finger up the strings. You will hear as many as 8 or 9 different notes (pitches) on each chord. Think of these as individual melody strings (notes) rather than parts of a chord.

Next, press the G7 chord and stroke intermittently up the strings; then the F chord. Stroke in different octaves as you change chords one after the other, in any order you choose. Hear how melodies start to emerge. You can actually play the song "Taps" on the C chord without even changing chords. Try it by ear. You can play the entire song starting on the 8th string, or move higher and start on the 19th.

To help you find melody more accurately, the 36 strings on the Autoharp are numbered from the lowest (1) to the highest (36).

fig 31: Numbered strings as they appear on the musical staff

Most Autoharps have a musical scale on the wide end under the strings (Fig. 32). The small white numbers printed in units of five will give you an indication of the specific area in which the melody string is located. You will press the proper chord bar and stroke up to the designated string number. Finding the melody is not difficult because several strings on either side of the melody string are automatically muted. You are aiming for a general location only. If you know the chord changes and string number you cannot make a mistake.

For those who have models without scale labels, cut out the Melody Aid® on p 167. Place it under the strings to the left side of the chord bars. Move it into position with the heavy line under the lowest string, and fasten it on one end with tape (see Fig. 36).

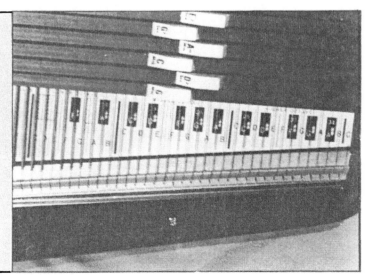

Fig. 32 Scale Label

Fig. 33

Stroking on this side allows you to see the scale label and its numbers more clearly.

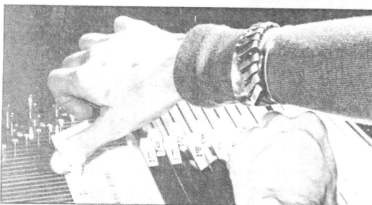

Fig. 34

Using a thumb pick and "crossing over"

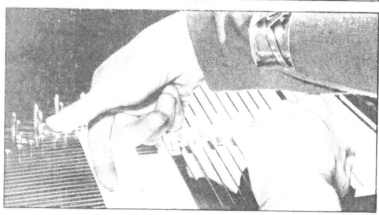

Fig. 35

Using the index finger

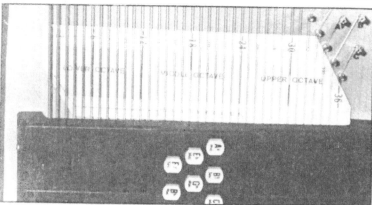

Fig. 36

Appalachian Style
with Melody Aid attached.

Now, play the complete version of Swanee River, following the chord changes shown above the music. Two more chords have been added for color. Remember, each number indicates the location of the melody note (string). Start your stroke about 10 strings below this and continue up to the melody string. The proper chord in which that melody string is located is placed above the number. The chord symbol is not repeated until time for a new chord to be played.

The slash / means to repeat the previous melody note and chord. An arrow ⟋ is a gentle upstroke played with the thumb in the lower octave to keep the beat going.

SWANEE RIVER

This next song has a definite pattern to the melody as is true of rounds. The first two bars are repeated in a higher octave; then some fast changes occur using the three principal chords of C in rapid sequence; the final bar is the same as the first.

You may have discovered the more frequent use of the 7th chord* of the key in which the song is written. It is in this chord that many of the non-chord tones (melody notes not part of the accompanying chord) are found.

See how much more interesting melody strumming is when applied to the first "one chord" song in this book.

*See p. 163 for a discussion of chords and chord groupings.

THREE BLIND MICE

Chords used: C, F, & G7

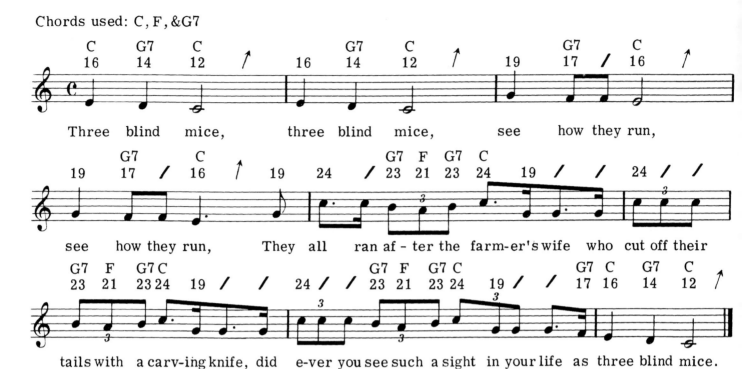

Three blind mice, three blind mice, see how they run,

see how they run, They all ran af-ter the farm-er's wife who cut off their

tails with a carv-ing knife, did e-ver you see such a sight in your life as three blind mice.

Here are two more rounds which lend themselves to melody strumming.

OH, HOW LOVELY IS THE EVENING

Chords used: D, G, and A7

Oh how love — ly is the eve — ning,

is the eve — ning, when the bells are

sweet — ly sing — ing, sweet — ly sing — ing

Ding Dong, Ding Dong Ding Dong...

54

This next song can be played with only one chord (Dm) as a simple round, but needs more chords for melody strumming. It is played in the key of D minor. Principal chords are: Dm, Gm & A7

SHALOM CHAVERIM

Israeli Folk Song

Chords used: Dm, Gm, A7, & C

Sha - lom Cha-ve-rim Sha - lom Cha-ve-rim Sha - lom   Sha - lom   L'

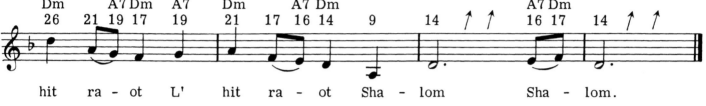

hit   ra - ot   L'   hit   ra - ot   Sha - lom   Sha - lom.

For the the final song in melody strumming play this old spiritual. After playing the first verse experiment and see how the melody can be played an octave higher, starting on the 28th string. It's a little too high to sing, but will make a fine Autoharp duet. I'm sure by now you can pick out the tune by ear!

Notice that the melody note in measures 9, 10, & 11 is the same, but the chords are different. This shows that the "back up" harmony is as important as the correct melody note. It also teaches the student something about the composition of various chords, and notes they have in common.*

JACOB'S LADDER

Chords used: C, F, G7, & G, C7

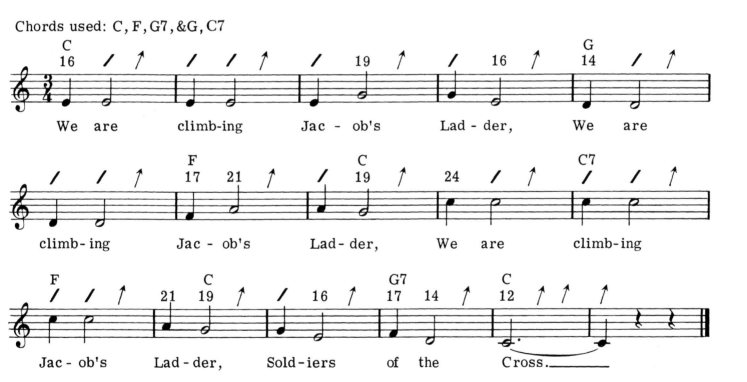

We are   climb-ing   Jac - ob's   Lad - der,   We are

climb- ing   Jac - ob's   Lad - der,   We are   climb-ing

Jac - ob's   Lad - der,   Sold-iers   of   the   Cross._____

2. Rise, shine give God glory, (3)
   Soldiers of the Cross.

3. Every rung goes higher, higher, (3)
   Soldiers of the Cross.

4. Sinner, do you love your Jesus? (3)
   Soldiers of the Cross.

5. If you love Him, why not serve Him, (3)
   Soldiers of the Cross.

*See pp. 64 & 65 of "Teaching Music With The Autoharp," Nye-Peterson, for "Jacob's Ladder" arranged for enriched harmony (6th and 9th chords).

55

LESSON 14: MELODY PICKING

In melody picking, press down the designated chord and pinch gently with the thumb and index, or thumb and middle finger in the area of the melody note (string). You are not plucking an open string, but pinching the correct section of the depressed chord. In melody strumming you stroked up to the melody string.

In melody picking the index or middle finger plucks the string. The position of the thumb is optional: wider apart for more depth of sound, and closer for faster picking.

Thumb and finger picks are not essential, but will produce a louder tone (See Fig. 8 p. 13).

Begin by pressing the C chord and gently pinching with the thumb and index finger in intervals up the strings.

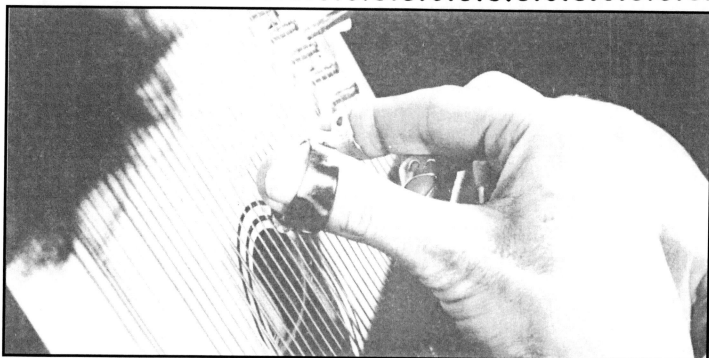

Fig. 37 Hand ready to pinch

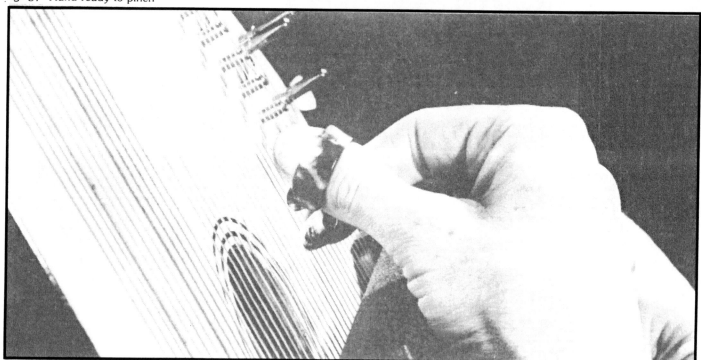

Fig. 38 Completed pinch

Notice that the thumb and index finger come together less than an inch above the strings. Try to hit only one string with your index finger and one or two with your thumb. Be sure not to drag your fingers together heavily or the sound will be scratchy and unpleasant.

The following songs can be played on the Autoharp on your lap or on the table, but Appalachian style is recommended.

The chord symbols and numbers are the same as in melody strumming. However, the numbers will refer to the placement of the index or middle finger on the strings and the chord symbols and slashes will indicate a pinch.

The next song can be played in two sections of the Autoharp. Use small pinches with the thumb and index finger on the first verse, and wider pinches with the thumb and middle finger for the second. The thumb still sounds the bass strings, so the pinch must be wider to play the higher strings at the same time.

ALL THROUGH THE NIGHT

night... While the wear - y world is sleep - ing

all through the night. O'er thy spir - it

gent - ly steal - ing, Vi - sions of de - light re-veal - ing,

Breathes a pure and hol - y feel - ing all through the night.

This next song is greatly enriched when played with dulcimer, recorder and any of the older musical instruments.

THE ASH GROVE

English Song

Chords used: F, Bb, C7, Dm, Gm, D7, G7, C, A7, & F7

Down yon - der green val - ley where stream-lets me -

an - der, When twi - light__ is__ fad - ing I

pen - sive - ly roam. Or at the bright

noon - tide in sol - i - tude__ wan - der, A -

mid the__ dark__ shades of the lone - ly ash grove. 'Twas

there while__ the__ black - bird was cheer - ful - ly__

sing - ing, I first met__ that__ dear one, the

joy of my heart, A - round as for__

glad - ness the blue - bells__ were ring - ing, Ah!

then lit - tle__ thought I how soon we should part.

2. Still glows the bright sunshine o'er valley and mountain,
Still warbles the blackbird its note from the tree;
Still trembles the moonbeam on streamlet and fountain,
But what are the beauties of nature to me?

With sorrow, deep sorrow, my bosom is laden,
All day I go mourning in search of my love.
Ye echoes! Oh, tell me, where is the sweet maiden?
"She sleeps 'neath the green turf down by the Ash Grove."

Many spirituals, gospel hymns, and Christmas songs lend themselves well to melody picking. Since melody picking is more brilliant when played in the higher octaves, many of the following songs that are pitched high are best performed as instrumentals.

GO TELL IT ON THE MOUNTAIN

Chords used: G , C ,&D7, A7

2. While shepherds kept their watching;
   O'er wand' ring flocks by night;
   Behold! From out the Heavens,
   There shown a holy light.
   (Chorus: Go, tell it, etc.)

THE MORE WE GET TOGETHER

Chords used: F, B♭, & C7

IN THE EVENING

Chords used: G, C, D7, G7, A7, & E7

In the eve-ning by the moon-light you can hear those voi-

ces sing-in'___ In the eve-ning by the moon-light

you can hear those ban-jos ring-in'___ How the

old folks would en-joy it They would

sit all night and list-en___ As we sang in the

eve-ning by the moon-light.

LESSON 15: MELODY PICKING WITH THUMB BRUSHES

The thumb has a double function in melody picking. It is part of the initial pinch, and also provides the necessary rhythm accompaniment. This is a difficult movement to do correctly. It is a gentle up and down brushing ⤴⤵ with the thumb, usually in the lower octave. It takes place after a pinch, and fills in the "spaces" of the melody. It is a rotating wrist motion. The thumb is kept straight and does not wiggle. Do not scrub or scratch the strings; barely touch them. These thumb strokes are only an accompaniment and should not overpower the melody.

Fig. 39 Pinch-thumb-brush stroke.

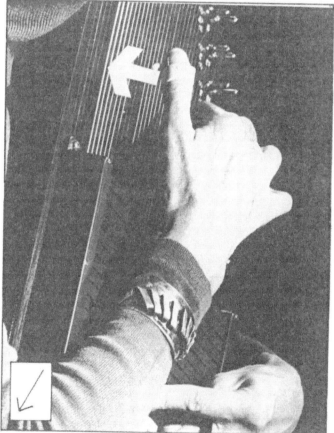

THUMB BRUSH

Practice this motion, saying as you do it: "Pinch, up-down, up-down; Pinch, up-down, up-down." Notice how your thumb opens up on the final downstroke, ready to pinch again. Speed it up, until you can say: "Pinch, up-down, Pinch, up-down" rapidly, several times.

You are now ready to play "Little Brown Jug." Observe how the brushes sometimes are used instead of a pinch (over "live" and "in a").

63

LITTLE BROWN JUG

Chords used: C, F, G7, &C7

Thumb brushes are used the same way in this next old folk song of English origin. They can be substituted many times for regular melody pinches, depending on how skillful you become. When used this way the thumb will carry the melody.

There are two arrangements of this song. The first is straight folk style, and the second uses an unusual harmonization which carries out the Elizabethan feeling of the song.

THE RIDDLE SONG
(Arrangement #1)

Chords used: F, B♭, &C7

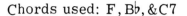

I gave my love a cher-ry that had no stone. I

gave my love a chick-en that had no bone. I

gave my love a sto-ry that had no end. I

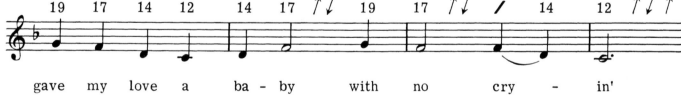

gave my love a ba-by with no cry - in'

2. How can there be a cherry that has no stone?
How can there be a chicken that has no bone?
How can there be a story that has no end?
How can there be a baby with no cryin'?

3. A cherry, when it's blooming, it has no stone.
A chicken, when it's pipping, it has no bone.
The story that I love you, it has no end.
A baby, when it's sleeping, has no cryin'.

THE RIDDLE SONG
(Arrangement #2)

Chords used: F, Bb, C, Dm, Am, &Gm

I gave my love a cher - ry that had no

stone. I gave my love a chick - en that

had no bone. I gave my love a

sto - ry that had no end. I

gave my love a ba - by with no cry - in'.

Notice how the 7th chords are not used in this arrangement.
Also, the song ends on a C chord, which, unlike the majority of
songs, is not a key chord.

A final example of using thumb brushes for rhythm accompaniment is:

SKIP TO MY LOU

Chords used: D&A7

1. Lost my part - ner what'll I do? Lost my part - ner

what'll I do? Lost my part - ner

what'll I do? Skip to my Lou my

dar - ling Lou, Lou, skip to my Lou,

Lou, Lou, skip to my Lou Lou, Lou,

skip to my Lou, skip to my Lou my dar - ling.

LESSON 16: MELODY PICKING: PINCHES AS "FILLER" STROKES

There are numerous ways to fill the pauses in a melody. They are almost always combined with some variation of the thumb-brush technique just learned (thumb-brushes in the middle or higher octave; alternating up and down-strokes with the thumb and index finger; or rhythmic strokes with the Loose Fist).

In the next song small ascending pinches with the thumb and index finger and the thumb and middle finger provide an ongoing beat and make your style more interesting. *The pinches are indicated by the small notes between phrases.*

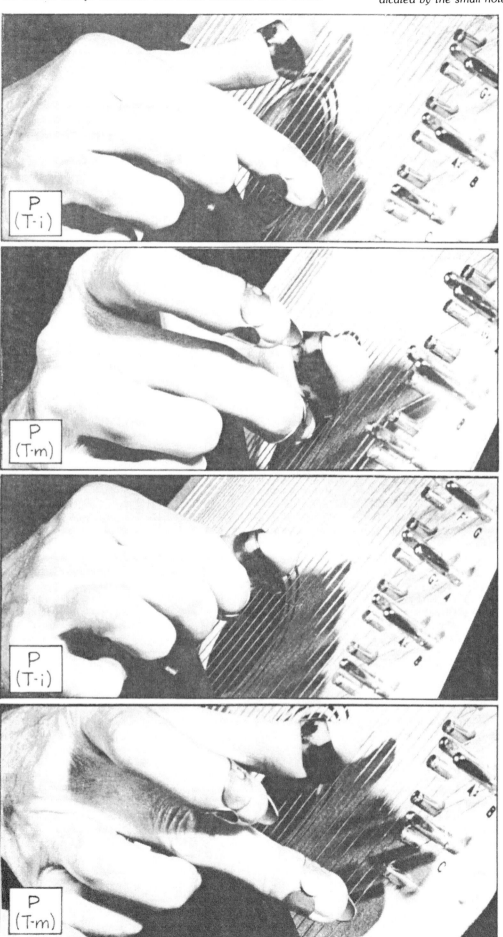

Fig. 40 Small ascending pinches

LONESOME VALLEY

Now, reverse the pinches and go from the higher to the lower strings between pauses in the melody. An effective way to pinch backwards is to start off in the higher octave with a thumb and middle finger pinch, followed by one using the thumb and index finger, then the thumb and middle finger. Keep alternating the pinches according to the number you need, and you'll find that you can execute them with greater speed and smoothness than if you just use the thumb and index finger. You can also try this same technique on the ascending as in Fig. 40.

BURY ME NOT ON THE LONE PRAIRIE

Chords used: D, G, A7, & (A)

2. Oh, bury me not on the lone prairie,
   Where coyotes howl and the wind blows free.
   In a narrow grave just six by three.
   Oh, bury me not on the lone prairie."

3. "It matters not I've oft been told,
   Where the body lies when the heart grows cold
   Yet grant, oh grant this wish to me:
   Oh, bury me not on the lone prairie."

4. "I've always wished to be laid when I died
   In the little churchyard on the green hillside.
   By my father's grave there let mine be,
   And bury me not on the lone prairie."

5. "Oh, bury me not" and his voice failed there,
   But we took no heed of his dying prayer.
   In a narrow grave just six by three
   we buried him there on the lone prairie.

6. And the cowboys now as they roam the plain,
   For they marked the spot where his bones were lain,
   Fling a handful of roses o'er his grave
   With a prayer to Him who his soul will save.

In the next old gospel song combine ascending and descending pinches or create your own filler strokes.

I'VE GOT PEACE LIKE A RIVER

Lively, joyful tempo

Chords used: G, C, D7, &A7

2. I've got joy like a fountain, etc.

3. I've got love like an ocean, etc.

LESSON 17: MELODY PICKING USING TRAVIS STRUMS AND HAMMERIN' ON

Travis strums can be used to create a country sound when playing melody. In this next old love ballad, Travis strum #13 (p.45) is used very effectively. The pattern looks like this:

The thumb will stroke each melody string and the alternating index and middle fingers will provide a rhythm accompaniment. The strum is shown over the first few bars of music only, but must be continued throughout the piece. Be sure to hit a different section of the specified octave on each stroke.

CARELESS LOVE

Chords used: G, C, D7, G7, & A7

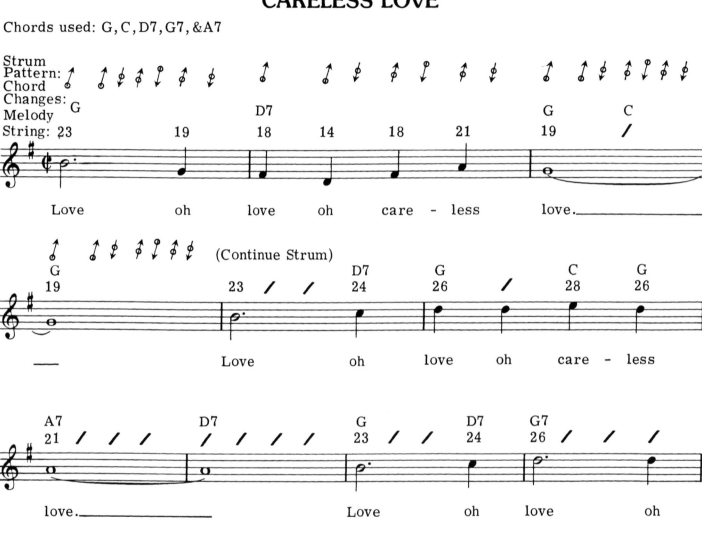

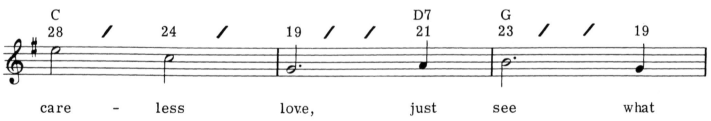

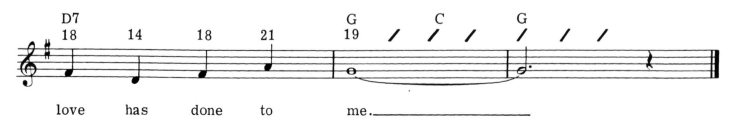

Change the previous pattern, slightly, to have the middle finger play on the first "off beat" rather than the index finger. It will look like this:

1   2   &   3   &   4   &

T   T   m   T   i   T   m

Basically, the pattern goes from the higher to the lower octave, whereas the previous one worked from the lower to the higher. Remember, to fit the pattern with the melody there will be an *upstroke on each melody note with the thumb.*

After you have learned the strum, add an adaptation of the

guitar technique called "hammerin' on." Ⓗ

Using the thumb, loose fist, or fingernail of the index finger, gently brush the open strings of the middle octave before the chord has been depressed. Once the strings have sounded, immediately press the proper chord bar. This gives an "ah-um" effect very common in country and bluegrass playing. Sometimes this stroke is done very rapidly and sometimes more slowly, depending on the mood of the song. However, it should be used sparingly, as is true of any special effect. Naturally, the hammerin' on stroke will take the place of the first upstroke in the Travis pattern.

YELLOW ROSE OF TEXAS

Chords used: C, F, & G7

This type of picking is used by many bluegrass Autoharp players and is a good introduction to the fast strumming in the next lesson. On "Wildwood Flower" play "hammerin' on" with a pinch (played with the thumb and index finger), combined with both melody picking and the previous Travis strum. The two melody notes after each Ⓗ stroke are pinched; thus the second pinch takes the place of the first thumb stroke in the Travis pattern. As you practice, you'll see how this fits with the melody. Varying your style this way always makes your performance more interesting.

WILDWOOD FLOWER

Bluegrass Song

Chords used: C, F, &G7

1. I'll en - twine and I'll min - gle my ra - ven black
2. Oh he prom - ised to love me, He called me his

hair_____ with the ros - es so
flow'r,_____ Lit - tle flow'r of the

red and the li - lies so fair._____
wild - wood to cheer ev - 'ry hour,_____

I a - woke from my dream and my
And I'll pray night and day he'll re -

i - dol was clay, His wild - wood flow - er
gret this dark hour, When he, my love, dis -

fad - ed, He threw it a - way._____
card - ed His frail wild - wood flow'r._____

For those who wish more practice in this kind of melody picking, try Grandfather's Clock (p. 144), and Oh, Dem Golden Slippers (p. 49) and Long, Long Ago (p. 45). You can add the melody chord changes, using the three principal chords of the key in which the song is written.

LESSON 18: MELODY PICKING, BLUEGRASS STYLE

Bluegrass music has its own unique sound, which originated in the Southeastern area of the United States. It evolved from three finger picking perfected in the 1940's by Earl Scruggs and Bill Monroe, the "Father of Bluegrass."

A typical bluegrass ensemble includes dobro guitar, 5-string banjo, fiddle, guitar, bass, and Autoharp. Rarely, if ever, are instruments electrified, and there is usually only one of each instrument in the group. As is customary, each person will take his turn at an instrumental solo, or "break." The other instruments will "back up," or accompany, him, without competing for the melody. After his "break," the player will then back up the next soloist with an interesting and delicate strum.

It is important, therefore, that you learn not only intricate and fast melody picking, but also master the many mountain strums presented earlier in this book. For other suitable bluegrass rhythmic patterns see a discussion of banjo rolls on p.146.

Typical bluegrass melody picking is done in the middle or higher octaves, just as much of the singing is of the high tenor quality. The thumb and index finger alternate in playing the melody, with the thumb taking the upstrokes and playing most of the melody notes, and the index finger filling in the rhythm with downstrokes. Add to this an alternating thumb (between the lower and middle octave) and you have the foundation for fast, exciting Autoharp. There are also all kinds of variations and special effects used in bluegrass, such as drag notes, back slurs, and hammerin' on. These will be discussed in the next lesson.

On the following song use only the thumb and index finger. To get you started, T or i will be indicated above the melody chords and string numbers. Once you have the technique mastered this will not be necessary.

Remember, in *bluegrass:* T = an upstroke on the melody string with the thumb, or an occasional rhythm beat

i = a downstroke on the melody string with the index finger, or a downstroke with the index finger to keep the rhythm going

This music is so fast when played correctly that it would be virtually impossible, and very clumsy, to use thumb strokes or pinches for every melody note. The notes, or strings, are often very close together, and the thumb and index finger have to work with great accuracy to get the thin, almost single string sound of this type of music.

Be sure to wear a thumb and finger pick (See Fig. 8 , p.13). It gives that authentic "twangy" quality as well as clearer definition of melody.

ARKANSAS TRAVELER

Chords used: G, C, D7, & A7

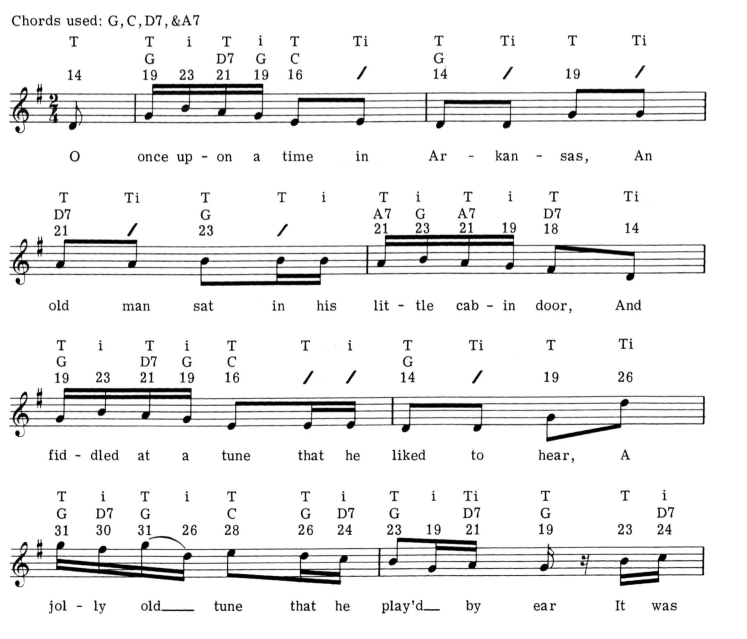

75

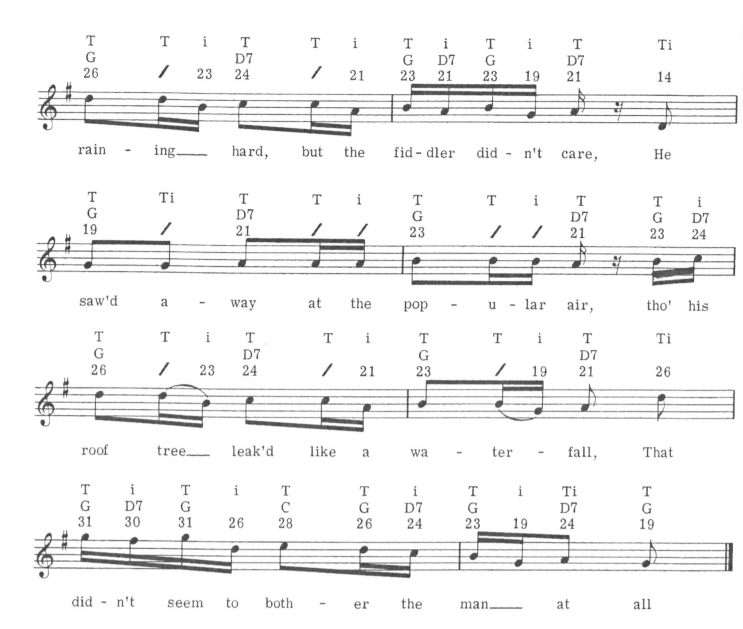

rain - ing___ hard, but the fid-dler did-n't care, He

saw'd a - way at the pop - u - lar air, tho' his

roof tree___ leak'd like a wa - ter - fall, That

did-n't seem to both - er the man___ at all

2. A traveler was riding by that day,
   And stopped to hear him a-practicing away;
   The cabin was afloat and his feet were wet,
   But still the old man didn't seem to fret.
   So the stranger said, "Now the way it seems to me,
   You'd better mend your roof, "said he.
   But the old man said, as he played away,
   "I couldn't mend it now, it's a rainy day."

3. The traveler replied: "That's all quite true,
   But this, I think, is the thing for you to do;
   Get busy on a day that is fair and bright,
   Then patch the old roof till it's good and tight."
   But the old man kept on a-playing at his reel,
   And tapp'd the ground with his leathery heel:
   "Get along,", said he, "for you give me a pain;
   My cabin never leaks when it doesn't rain."

> Other fast songs that lend themselves to this style are: "Polly
> Wolly Doodle" (p. 22), "Hard, Ain't It Hard" "Do Lord"
> (p. 30), "Cindy" (p. 28), "Red River Valley" (p. 19), and "Dixie"
> (p. 34). Practice at least one of them. This will be a challenge,
> since you'll have to find the melody chords and fit the thumb and
> index finger strokes into the chord changes.

LESSON 19: BLUEGRASS STYLE MELODY PICKING WITH DRAG NOTES

Drag notes are similar to Hammerin' On, except that the stroke is slower, louder, and covers more open strings before the chord bar is depressed. The effect is an upward slur to a higher pitch.

The thumb is literally dragged over three to five open strings before reaching the melody string. In very fast playing there will only be time to stroke a couple strings. In slower, more deliberate songs, more strings can be sounded. The melody picking technique is the same as in the previous song. This time, however, the T and i strokes will only be written over the first line of music. You fill in the rest.

GO TELL AUNT RHODY

Chords used: G&D7

Go, tell Aunt Rho - dy, Go tell aunt Rho - dy
(Continue Strum)

Go, Tell Aunt Rho - dy the old gray goose is dead.

2. The one she's been saving(three times)
   To make a feather bed.

3. She died in the mill pond(three times)
   A standin' on her head.

4. The goslins are mournin'(three times)
   Because their mother's dead,

*(Dr) = Drag notes

Instruction Cassette ($9.98) and Tuning Cassette ($8.98) to use with this book are available from the publisher or by writing Meg Peterson, 33 S. Pierson Road, Maplewood, NJ 07040.

OH, SUSANNA

Chords used: C, F, G7, &G

Try this same drag stroke in place of hammerin' on (H) on the melodies in Lesson 17.

LESSON 20: BLUEGRASS MELODY PICKING: COMBINING BACK SLURS AND DRAG NOTES:

A back slur (Bsl) is the opposite of a drag note (Dr). Instead of slurring upward in pitch, you start several strings higher than the melody note and drag downward over the open strings using the index finger. When the melody string is reached, depress the proper chord bar and continue melody picking using alternate T and i strokes.

SOURWOOD MOUNTAIN

Chords used: G, C, & D7

* (Bsl) = Back Slur

79

On the second verse try using hammerin' on (H) (p.73), pinching with the thumb and index finger, in place of the back slur. Pinch on the open strings and immediately depress the chord bar. Notice how different this effect is, since the thumb will be pinching a few lower notes, adding depth to the sound.

This driving beat with its high pitched finger picking gives a drone-like sound, almost like the Scottish songs, as does this next tune. Here we combine the back slur and drag notes.

On the verse the melody and back slurs are played by the index finger in a strong downstroke toward the lower strings. In this instance, the thumb is providing the rhythm accompaniment. On the chorus, switch to the thumb which will play upstrokes for the drag notes and the melody. For variety, alternate octaves on the chorus, playing once in the higher octave as written, and the next time in the lower octave. It will be a hard-driving beat, adding to the haunting quality of this modal tune. Notice that the chords used are not the typical principal chords in the key of G, but those characteristic of the Mixolydian mode. No sharps are required in this piece.

OLD JOE CLARK

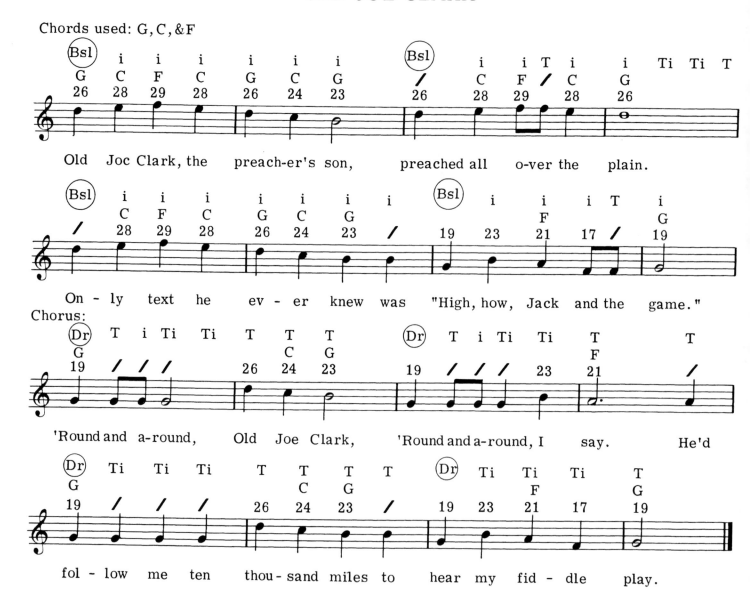

2. I used to live on the mountain top,
But now I live in town.
I'm boarding at the big hotel,
Courting Betsy Brown. Chorus.

4. Old Joe had a yeller cat,
She would not sing or pray.
She stuck her head in a buttermilk jar.
And washed her sings away. Chorus.

3. Wish I was a sugar tree,
Standing in the town.
Every time a pretty girl passed,
I'd shake some sugar down. Chorus.

5. Wish'd I had my own sweetheart,
I'd set her on a shelf,
And every time she smiled at me,
I'd get up there myself. Chorus.

Other songs which can be practiced using bluegrass back slurs, hammerin' on, and drag notes are "Camptown Races" (p145), "Darling Corey", "She'll Be Comin' 'Round the Mountain" (p. 50), "Bile Them Cabbage Down", and "Calton Weaver" (p.31).

RHYTHM PICKING

The following 27 lessons build on the previous 13 basic strums and incorporate a wide variety of different rhythms and styles. There are fewer chord changes than in melody picking and no more numbers under the chord designations. The techniques set forth draw heavily upon guitar and banjo right hand picking, without the need to hit exact strings, only approximate areas of each octave. The combinations of strokes are infinite within each general category.

LESSON 21: CALYPSO

Calypso music originated in Trinidad, but had its roots in the polyrhythms and music of both Spain and Africa. It has become the musical trademark of the West Indies and, along with reggae, its latest offshoot from Jamaica, has greatly influenced the rock scene.

Calypso music is repetitive, often in call-and-response style, and the lyrics can be about any subject, no matter how ordinary. Its rhythmic characteristic is *syncopation*. This means that the natural accent is moved to a beat not usually stressed, namely the upbeat (or second half) of the 2nd beat. At the same time the 3rd beat is omitted, or repressed. This produces an irregularity of rhythm not found in most American folk songs. Often, in an effort to make the lyrics fit this rhythm the emphasis is placed on a syllable not normally stressed.

To practice this rhythm, divide a bar into eight parts, *accenting* (>) the first and fourth beats. Start by clapping the rhythm evenly and counting:

ONE - and - two - AND - three - and - four - and

Next play the rhythm, using the thumb and index finger in the lower and middle octaves.

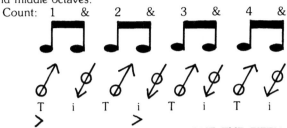

When you can play this evenly, LEAVE OUT THE FIFTH STROKE and you have this syncopated pattern:

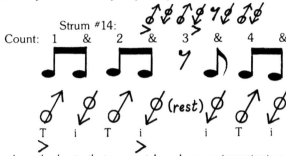

Remember, the beats that are *not heard* are as important as those that are played, so be sure to remain silent when it is indicated, and *keep accenting the first and fourth strokes.*

WATER COME A ME EYE

Chords used: C&G7

Moderately slow

Jamaican Folk Song

Ev - 'ry time I think of Li - za, Wa-ter come a me eye.

Ev - 'ry time I think of Li - za, Wa-ter come a me eye.

Refrain:

Come back, Li - za, Come back girl, Wa-ter come a me eye.

Come back, Li - za, Come back girl, Wa-ter come a me eye.

Strum #14a:

To add variety to this strum, add the middle finger in a modified Travis pattern, keeping the same rhythm. Be sure the thumb hits a slightly different section of the strings on each of its strokes.

Chords used: C, F, G7, & (Dm)

MATILDA

Moderately slow

Chorus

Ma - til - da_____ Ma - til - da_____

(Continue Strum)

— Ma - til - da she take me mon - ey and

Last time Fine

run Ven - e - zue - la._____

1. Five
2. My

Verse

thou - sand dol - lars friend I lost
mon - ey was to buy me house and land, The

wo - man ev - en take me cart and hoss; Ma - til - da she
wo - man she got a seri - ous plan; Ma - til - da she

D.C. al Fine

take me mon - ey and, Run Ven-e-zue - la._____
take me mon - ey and, Run Ven-e-zue - la._____

LESSON 22: CALYPSO: RASGUEADO

The next strum uses a type of guitar picking associated with the classical guitar, called the Rasqueado (pronounced ras- gay- ah-doh). It is a series of rapid finger strokes over the entire body of strings, starting with the little finger in the lower octave and moving toward the higher. Each finger brushes the string in quick succession, ending with the thumb. It is a flowing, gentle sound, best executed without picks. As your hand unfolds the fingernails will act as picks.

Fig. 41. Diagram of hand position during rasqueado.

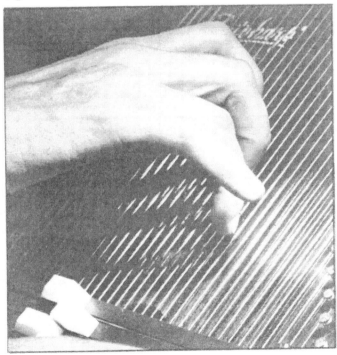

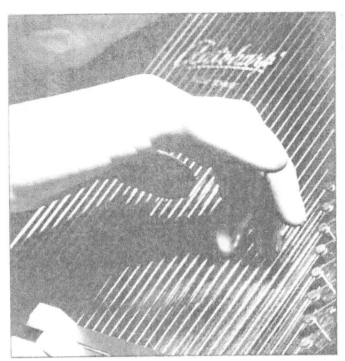

The symbol for rasqueado is R. Combined with finger strokes the strum looks like this. 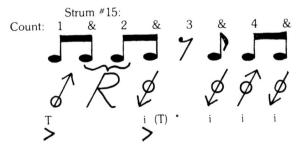 Notice how the timing in this and the next four Calypso strums is identical.

Strum #15:

*This stroke can be played with either the thumb or index finger. Optional strokes are always in parenthesis.

The next tune is a "digging" or work song from Jamaica. There are several versions of it, depending on the job involved. The singer might enjoy improvising his or her own verses related to a particular activity or subject.

83

BANANA BOAT LOADER'S SONG

Chords used: G, C, & D7

Chorus: (Continue Strum)

Day Oh Day— Oh Day da light an' me wan' go home

1. Come Mis-ter Tall-y-man, come tall-y me ba-na-na

Day da light an' me wan' go home.

2. Six hand, sev-en hand, eight hand bunch! shout!
3. We load ba-na-nas till the ear-ly light.
4. Some men work some men make love.

Six hand, sev-en hand, eight hand bunch! shout!
sleep all day and work all night.
we load ba-na-na while the moon a-bove.

D.S. 2 times al Coda

Day da light an' me wan' go home.

Coda

Day oh day— oh day da light an me wan' go home.

RASQUEADO WITH SLAP

Play the song, again, using a slight variation of the previous strum. Slap all the strings with the flat of your hand, instead of pausing, on the 3rd beat. This is especially effective when the pause occurs during a chord change as in the first two measures. The harmony will ring out even while the strings are being muf-fled. If the Autoharp is amplified the pattern is even more dramatic.

Fig. 42: Slap

Strum #15a:

Count: 1 & 2 & 3 & 4 &

T > i (T) i i i

*SI = Slap

RASGUEADO BACKWARDS

The rasgueado can also be played backwards, starting in the higher octave and drawing the four fingers down over the strings in rapid succession. As in all these calypso strums, the accent is on the 1st and 4th strokes. Picks could be used on this strum, since it is the fleshy part of the fingers and the thumb that touch the strings.

Strum #15b:
Count: 1   &   2   &   3   &   4   &

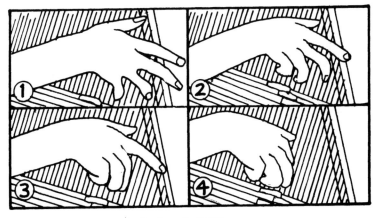

Fig. 43: Rasgueado Backwards (*RB)

The next song introduces two of the three principal chords in the key of Bb major. They are Bb, Eb, and F7.

EVERYBODY LOVES SATURDAY NIGHT

Key of Bb
Bb, Eb, & F7

Chords used: Bb & F7

Ev - 'ry-bod - y loves Sat - ur - day

Night._____ Ev - 'ry-bod - y

loves Sat - ur - day night._____

Ev - 'ry-bod - y, ev - 'ry-bod - y, ev - 'ry-bod - y,

ev - 'ry - bod - y, ev - 'ry - bod - y

loves Sat - ur - day night._____

Try the song once more, using a Slap (Sl) as in Strum #15a in place of the rest on the 3rd beat.

85

LESSON 23: CALYPSO: USING RING FINGER

This next strum is very similar to #15b, except that the back roll covers fewer strings, each note is more distinct, and only the ring, middle, and index fingers are used. The thumb plays in a slightly higher section on the 2nd beat, moving up, again, on the 4th beat.

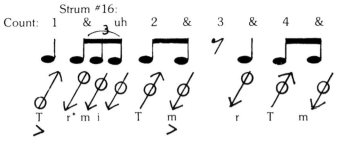

*r = Stroke with the ring finger.

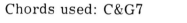

PAY ME MY MONEY DOWN

Chords used: C & G7

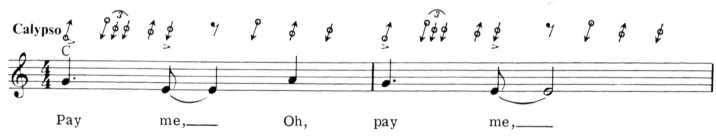

Pay me,___ Oh, pay me,___

Pay me my mon-ey down, Pay me or

go to jail,___ Pay me my mon-ey down.

Verse:

I wish I was Mis-ter Car-ter's son,___ Pay me my

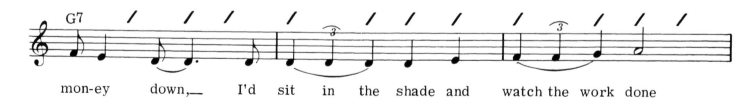

mon-ey down,___ I'd sit in the shade and watch the work done

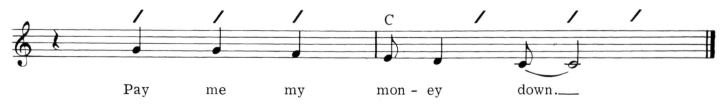

Pay me my mon - ey down.___

CALYPSO: USING ARPEGGIANDO STROKE

Now try the same song with a slightly different pattern and a backward arpeggiando ( ) (See p. 23). In this strum the arpeggiando stroke covers the two higher octaves and is played with the index finger.

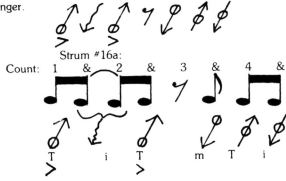

Strum #16a:

Count: 1 & 2 & 3 & 4 &

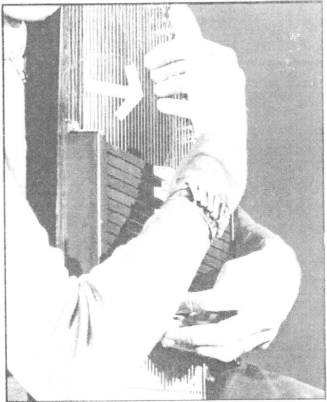

Fig. 45: Strum #16b

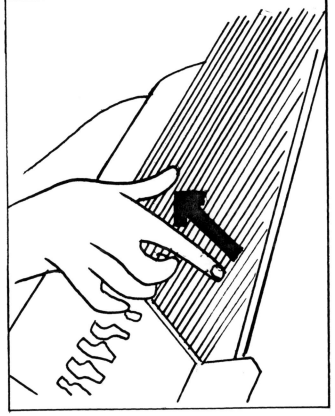

Fig. 44: Backward Arpeggiando

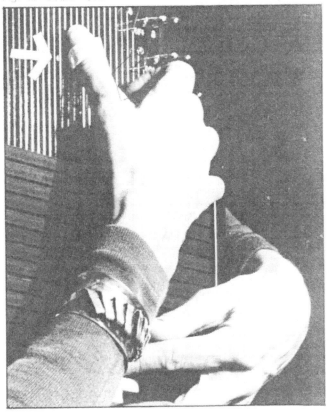

The next strum uses an upstroke arpeggiando( ) covering all the strings, and is played with a loose fist (LF). This is a very difficult pattern at first, since the thumb, which usually plays on the first beat of a piece, must now follow through rapidly on the second half of the first beat. The timing is essentially the same as the previous six strums, although there is no rest written under the third beat. The arpeggiando stroke can be stopped, but the strings will still continue to sound.

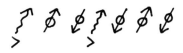

Strum #16b:

Count: 1 & 2 & 3 & 4 &

*The index finger can also be used for these short strokes.

THE SLOOP "JOHN B"

88

Send for the cap-tain a - shore, let me go home._____

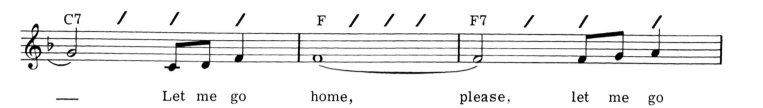

_____ Let me go home, please, let me go

home,_____ I feel so break up,

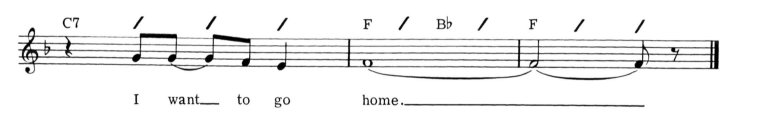

I want__ to go home._____

2. First mate he got sad; Feelin' awfully bad.
Captain come a-board, took him a-way.
Please let me a-lone, and let me go home,
Well, I feel so break up; I want to go home.
Chorus

3. Poor cook he got fits; And threw away all the grits.
Then he took and eat up all of the corn.
Please let me go home, I want to go home,
Well, this is the worst trip, since I was born.
Chorus

With more frequent chord changes this song can be a very exciting melody solo. Keep the syncopated strum pattern going
throughout and watch the tune emerge.

This Calypso pattern can also be used effectively with many
folk, pop, and rock songs such as "Rhinestone Cowboy," "Mary
Lou," "I'd Like To Teach The World To Sing," and "He's Got
The Whole World In His Hands." (p.15). Calypso songs for prac-
tice should be "Yellow Bird," "Jamaica Farewell," "Linstead
Market" (p.135), and "Round the Bay of Mexico."

LESSON 24: CALYPSO; ADVANCED STRUMS

You can think of the next pattern as having eight beats to the measure, or two groups of three strokes and one group of two strokes. Either way it gives a slight asymetrical feeling to the following tune and is about as easy at first as rubbing your stomach and patting your head!

Pinches with the thumb and middle finger (T-m) and the thumb and index finger (T-i) (p. 68 for illustrations of pinches) are done rapidly, accenting the 1st, 4th, and 7th strokes. The strokes written without arrows merely indicate the octave in which the pinch is played.

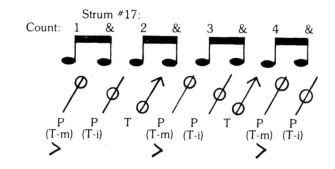

MARY ANN

Chords used: F&C7

All day, all night Ma-ry Ann_____

Down by the sea - shore sift-ing sand_____

Ev - en lit - tle child - ren__ love Ma-ry Ann,_____

'Cause she sings and dan - ces like no one can._____

The final Calypso strum is extremely difficult since the thumb is playing a downstroke on the second half of the first beat, rather than leading with an upstroke on the first beat. Practice the strum slowly on the previous song, then try it on any of the songs in this section. It is most effective when played rapidly and smoothly like a flamenco guitar strum. On the majority of strokes, the fingernails of the thumb, ring, and index fingers are used, so no picks are necessary. Notice how the rest is on the second rather than the third beat.

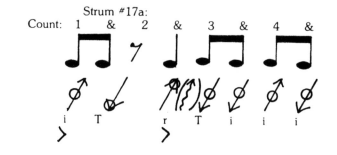

REGGAE: BLANKING OUT STROKE (Bl)

You can find calypso and reggae rhythms in many of the popular hits of today, from the music of Harry Belafonte, Johnny Nash, and Paul Simon, to the pure reggae songs of Bob Marley and Jimmy Cliff. Take the strums you have just mastered and use them to enjoy the music of your favorite artist.

To play reggae you would have to alter your strum, since the accent is predominantly on the 2nd and 4th beats. Try the next strum, using a new stroke (Bl) which blanks out all the strings by depressing three chord bars at once. Play the "one- and", then as you stroke on "two", press two chords simultaneously on either side of the designated chord to muffle the sound. Practice by saying "oom-a- chuck- a, oom- a-chuk- a," accenting the 2nd and 4th beats to get the reggae effect.

The fingers you use on the chord bars to blank out the sound will be the middle, ring, and index fingers if the Autoharp is on the table (Fig. 46).

Fig. 46 Using middle, ring, and index finger; 15 chord instrument.

There are several choices of fingering when the Autoharp is held Appalachian style, depending on the location of the chords to be blanked out and the strength of the player's fingers. Here are two alternatives:

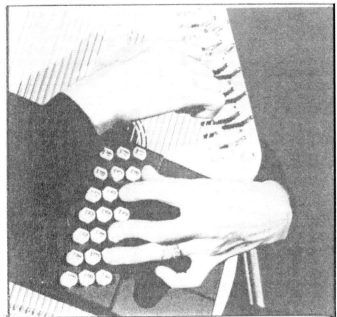

Fig. 47   Using middle, ring, and index finger
Appalachian style

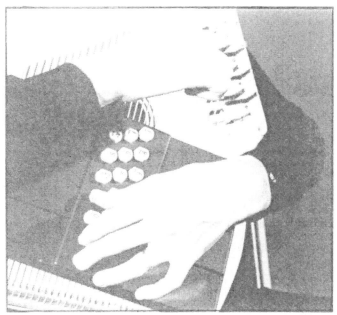

Fig. 48   Using index, thumb, and middle finger. Appalachian style

Fig. 49: Muting Bar

The 27 chord Caroler Chromaharp has a bar which, when pressed, mutes all the strings at once. This simplifies many calypso, reggae, and rock strums.

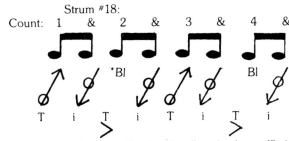

*Bl = Blanking out all strings. The thumb will stroke the muffled strings in the lower octave to keep the rhythm going.

Try this new pattern on a chord progression from an early Johnny Nash hit. Play the entire strum for each chord designation.

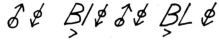

```
D - G - D - D
D - G - A - A
D - G - D - D
C - G - D - D
C - G - D - D
```

This type of stroke (Bl) can be incorporated into Travis picking, calypso rhythms, or pop and rock strums. It is especially effective when the Autoharp is amplified.

LESSON 25: FLAMENCO

Flamenco music is largely improvisatory. It brings forth images of Spanish gypsies, colorful dancing, exhausting tempos, and virtuoso classical guitar. Many of the calypso strums in the previous lessons, especially those featuring the rasqueado, can be used with flamenco. You can also make up your own song, using a typical chord sequence in the phrygian mode:

Am - G - F - E7`

The rhythmic pattern and chord progression are repeated over and over, as the tempo is increased, building up to a dramatic crescendo and coming to rest on the E7.

Try this next pattern, using the loose fist (LF) in the middle octave. Without picks the gentle scratching sound of the fingernails gives a flowing accompaniment to traditional flamenco. Notice how similar the pattern is to some of the mountain strums in lesson 9.

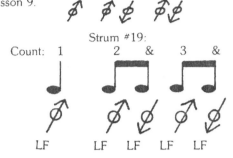

Use one complete strum per measure, increasing the tempo, or speed, to add to the excitement of the dance.

FLAMENCO DANCE

It's interesting to note that the chord progression in this piece is basically the same as the one used in the old English ballad "Greensleeves" (p125), but of course, the feeling and rhythmic pattern are entirely different. The progression starts on Dm instead of Am and goes like this: Dm - C - Bb - A7

The next strum is a two measure pattern, using Travis picking in the second measure. It is very powerful with a driving beat, and should be played with picks.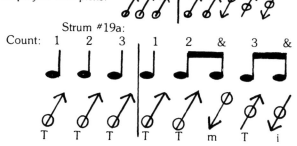

Try this on the previous song, using one complete pattern per measure.

A final strum to play with this dance uses three equal strokes on each beat, starting with the middle finger in the higher octave and ending with an upstroke with the thumb in the lower octave. It is similar in feeling to the rasgueado backwards (RB) on p. 85.

Practice the strum slowly at first, saying 1 da da, 2 da da, 3 da da, etc. Then speed up the tempo and use two complete patterns per measure.

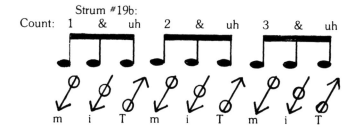

So far you've been playing 3/4 time. Now try this 4/4 strum, using the rasgueado (R) and no picks.

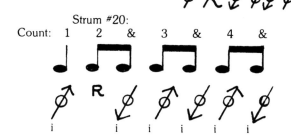

Notice that this next tune has a different chord progression. Use one strum pattern per measure.

FLAMENCO DANCE NO. 2

LESSON 26: RAGTIME

Ragtime, the music popular from the 1890's until the end of World War I, is having a revival in the 1970's. This style of music originated in the midwest with Scott Joplin as its most famous musician. It spread to New Orleans where "Jelly Roll" Morton took over, and on to New York where "Fats" Waller became one of its leading exponents, and Irvin Berlin's rinkydink show tunes were immediately popular.

Ragtime flourished during the days of the player piano, since it is, basically, a piano style. It is very rhythmic over a syncopated melody, the most common syncopation being an anticipated 3rd beat (similar to calypso).

Since ragtime tunes are mostly instrumentals with melodies too complicated for melody picking, and also, since they are often improvisatory, the Autoharp strums will only be accompanying chord progressions with varying rhythmic patterns. In the following strums, the thumb keeps a steady beat over the syncopated melody. To get warmed up, first try clapping these three rhythms, being sure to place the accent where indicated; then study the strum patterns that fit them.

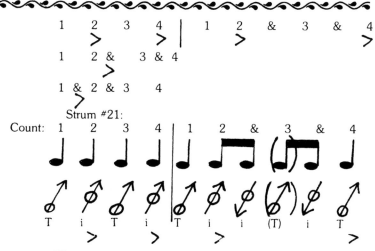

This is a two measure pattern and a forerunner of the Detroit sound (Motown), the rock 'n 'roll conception of the blues. Try it on the following chord sequence:

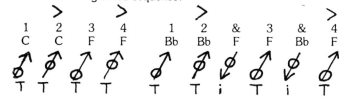

When the 3rd beat remains silent the pattern can be used very effectively on this Scott Joplin standard.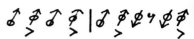

THE ENTERTAINER

(21 and 27 chord model)

Scott Joplin

Chords used: G, C, D7, G7, A7, C, & Cm

The next pattern employs the pinch with the thumb and middle finger. Everyone can hum the tune, again, or just play the chords as a progression.

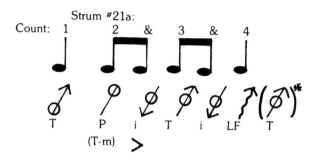

*This stroke can be substituted for the arpeggiando stroke, if preferred. It can be played with the thumb or index finger.

The final ragtime strum uses a modified Travis pattern with an accented brush stroke at the end. Notice how all these patterns are different, yet they still retain the steady beat with the thumb. They're all fairly difficult, too, since the chords frequently change in the middle of the strum pattern.

Try these patterns on other ragtime songs such as "The Maple Leaf Rag" and "At A Georgia Camp Meeting," and see how well they represent this type of music.

Then try the chorus of the tune that was the theme song of Teddy Roosevelt and the Rough Riders during their Cuba campaign.

THERE'LL BE A HOT TIME IN THE OLD TOWN TONIGHT

LESSON 27: BLUES; TRIPLET RHYTHM

The blues is a forerunner of jazz originating from black work songs and spirituals. It deals with the struggles, problems, humor, and everyday experiences of life. Although the blues emerged, commercially, in the early 1900's, it began years before, as a vocal style, in the southern countryside.

Most blues tunes fall into a 12 bar chord progression and have a smoother, less percussive rhythm and slower tempo than ragtime. Two early examples of this music were written by W. C. Handy*; "Memphis Blues" (1909), and the "St. Louis Blues," both published in 1912. This ushered in an era of blues singers in the '20's, led by Bessie Smith, who sang about despair, loneliness, sorrow, and unrequited love. The influence and endurance of this music will be obvious to anyone who listens to the jazz, country, and rock hits of today.

One of the foundations of the blues rhythm is the triplet form, used in the next strum. This means that three evenly spaced strokes are played on each beat. As you practice, count:

1 da da, 2 da da; or 1 & uh, 2 & uh, etc.

There are no octave designations on the pattern because it can be played with the thumb, flat pick, or loose fist (see fig. 18 and 19, p. 28) in either the lower or middle octave, depending on the intensity of the song.

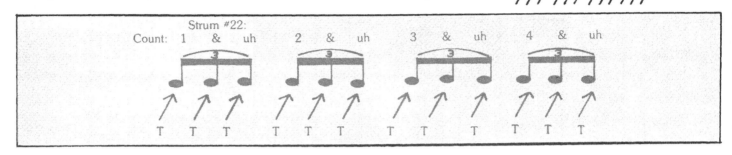

JELLY ROLL BLUES

*W. C. Handy was introduced to music by the Autoharp, before the turn of the century.

96

Here is a variation of Strum #22 which is easier to execute when playing fast blues songs. The rhythm is the same, but the triplets are played using up and down strokes with the index finger.

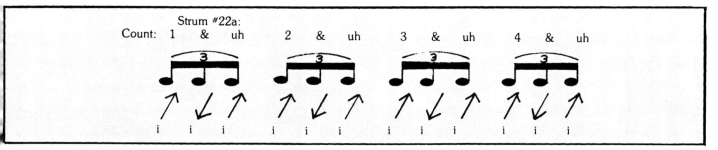

Try this pattern on a 16 bar blues, a standard, but less common form of the blues.

EASY RIDER

Chords used: G, C, D7, C7, & G7

Eas - y - Ri - der,   see   what   you   have   done,

— Oh   Lor - dy,   Eas -   Eas - y   Ri - der,—

see   what   you   have   done,   Well   you   made   me   love you,

now   your   man—   done   come.—————   And   it's

hey,   hey,   hey,   hey,   hey,   hey,   hey!—————

After you have perfected the two previous strums try a more advanced variation on both songs, using the thumb and index finger in the lower and middle octaves followed by a short Travis pattern on the 4th beat.

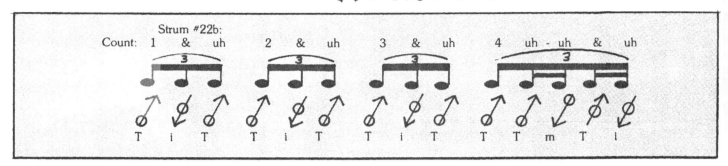

Now that you've learned all the difficult variations, try a final strum which simplifies the triplet and leads into the lesson on shuffle rhythm. As you sing the next song, think triplets, even when you have only one stroke per beat. Be sure to accent the "uh" on the 4th beat.

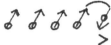

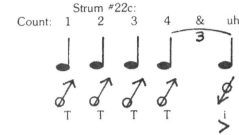

RAILROAD BILL

Chords used: C, F, G7, F7, E7, & D7

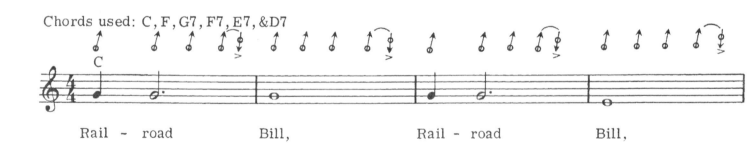

Rail - road   Bill,   Rail - road   Bill,

He nev - er worked and he nev - er   will, I'm gon - na

ride   old   Rail - road   Bill._____

LESSON 28: BLUES: SHUFFLE RHYTHM

Shuffle rhythm is played as if it were triplets with the middle note omitted.

On the Autoharp this rhythm is played as a straight up and down stroke in the middle octave using the thumb and index finger, loose fist, or flat pick.

As you practice say "tum - te - tum - te - tum," etc., accenting the shorter downstroke rather than the initial upstroke (Remember, downstroke does *not* mean down beat. The down beat in this case is on the upstroke, in Autoharp terminology).

Shuffle rhythm was used extensively by early rock musicians and gives a boogie-woogie flavor to the blues. There is a hesitation and improvisatory quality which makes it difficult to notate accurately. You must *feel* the blues.

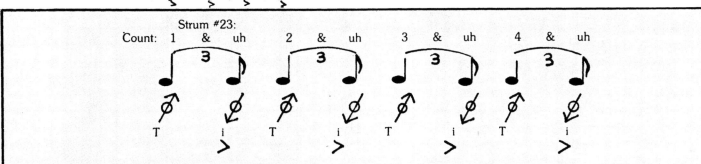

Use this strum on the following old blues melody. Notice how many 7th chords are used. The piece even ends on the 7th rather than the tonic chord. This increases the blues feeling.

JOE TURNER

2. He come with forty links of chain.
   He come with forty links of chian.
   Got my man and gone.

3. They tell me Joe Turner's come and gone.
   They tell me Joe Turner's come and gone.
   Done left me here to sing this song.

A variation of this pattern adds the lower octave with a return to the triplet figure on the 4th beat.

WORRIED MAN BLUES

Chords used: G, C7, D7, G7, (B7), & (Em)

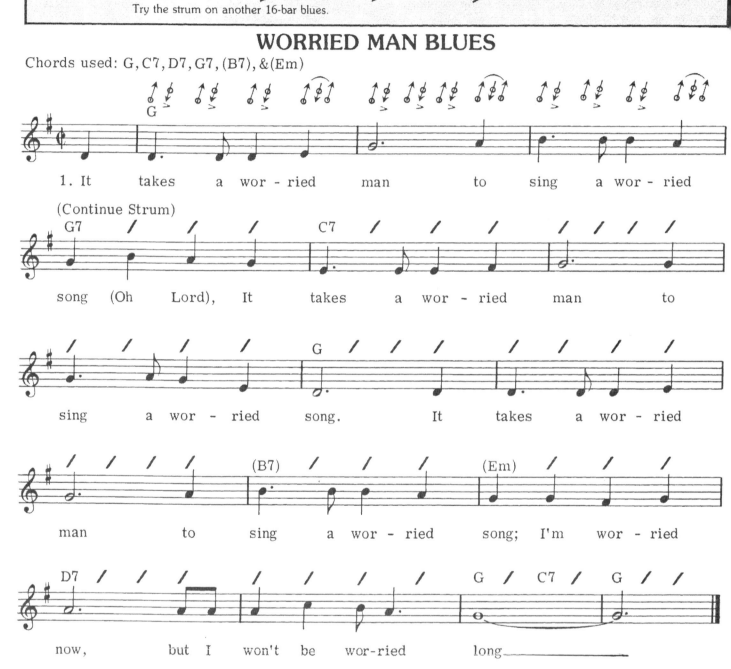

1. It takes a wor - ried man to sing a wor - ried

(Continue Strum)

song (Oh Lord), It takes a wor - ried man to

sing a wor - ried song. It takes a wor - ried

man to sing a wor - ried song; I'm wor - ried

now, but I won't be wor-ried long

2. I went across the river; and lay me down to sleep *(Repeat the first line twice*
   When I woke up, had shackles on my feet.

3. Twenty-nine links of chain around my leg,
   I couldn't get out no matter how I'd beg.

4. I asked that judge, tell me, what's gonna be my fine?
   Twenty-one years on the Rocky Mountain Line.

5. If anyone should ask you, who composed this song,
   Tell him 'twas I, and I sing it all day long.

An upstroke in the middle octave with the index finger, followed by a pinch with the thumb and middle finger, provides a fuller sound on the accent and a more driving beat. This strum is a real challenge, for the index finger is seldom used to start a pattern and may seem awkward at first. By now your fingers should be calloused enough so you won't need picks. Of course, the upstrokes are all done with the fingernail of the index finger.

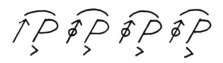

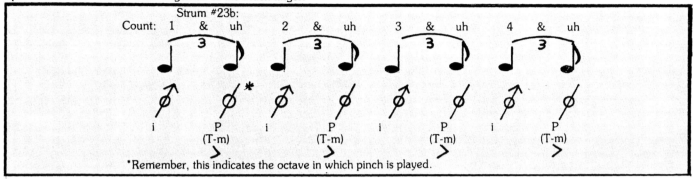

After this has been mastered, try leaving out the first part of the 2nd and 3rd beats, so there are three pinches in a row. This strum is good practice for the syncopated patterns introduced in the following lessons.

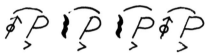

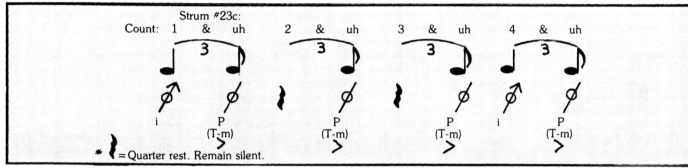

Now, try both of these strums on the next melody, written in the Mixolydian mode. The dissonances you get as you sing over the 7th chords add a haunting quality to the blues.

EVERY NIGHT WHEN THE SUN GOES IN

Chords used: C, F, G7, C7, F7, E7, Am, Dm, & (Em)

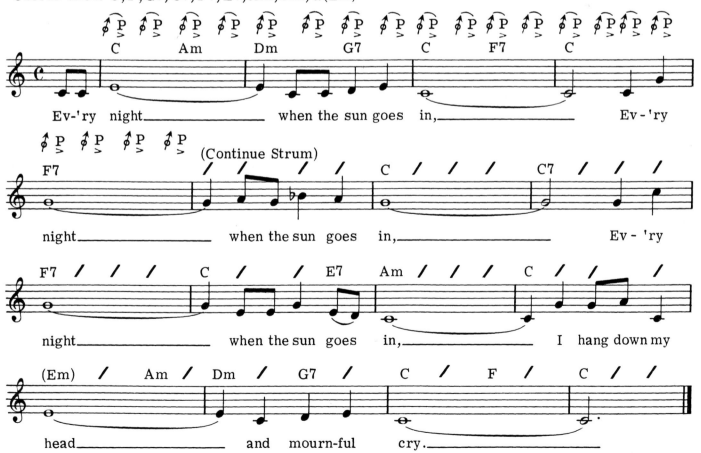

Several good practice songs for the shuffle rhythm are "Backwater Blues," "Crossroads Blues," "The Midnight Special," and "Goin' Down The Road Feelin' Bad" (p148).

101

LESSON 29: BLUES; DOUBLE THUMBING

Using the basic shuffle rhythm, move the thumb from the lower to the middle octave on beats "2" and "4". This is more pronounced than a straight alternating bass, for the thumb actually moves up and plays an upstroke in the same area where the index finger has just played a downstroke. Strokes are short, retaining the accent and hesitation necessary to create the blues effect.

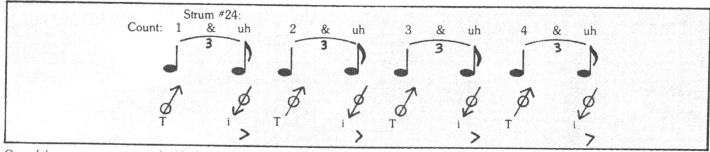

One of the many variations in double thumbing is to start in the middle (or lower) octave and have the alternating index finger move down to the area stroked by the thumb. The thumb, then, remains in the same octave. This affords a wide variety of combinations. You can experiment, using the middle as well as the index finger, alternating with the thumb.

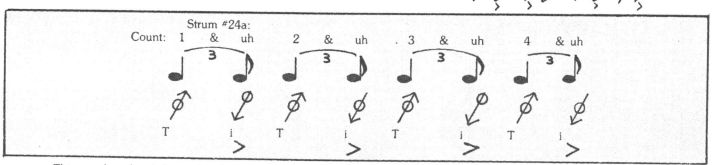

This song has already been played in melody picking style (p. 72). Now try it with these two strums as a straight blues ballad.

CARELESS LOVE

Chords used: D, G, A7, G7, D7, E7, & Gm

ROCKER STRUM

The rocker strum is very similar to double thumbing. However, in this particular rocker pattern the thumb and index finger move up the strings and down almost like a walking bass in boogie-woogie. The shuffle beat is maintained, and each stroke is played in a slightly different section of the specified octave. Strokes are short, covering only one or two strings.

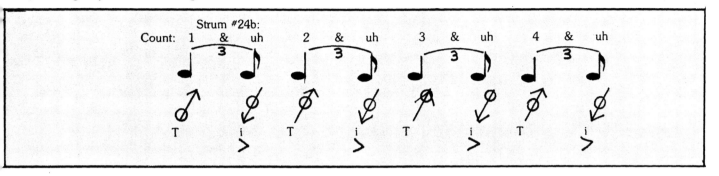

The next country blues ballad lends itself well to this rocker strum.

FRANKIE AND JOHNNY

Chords used: C, C7, F7, & G7

Frank-ie and John-ny were sweet-hearts; oh, Lord-y, how__ they could

love. Swore to be true__ to each oth-er, true as the stars a-

bove. He was her man,_____ but he done her wrong.__

SYNCOPATED STRUMS

This next strum has the same syncopated rhythm as the earlier calypso patterns, with a slightly different accent. It is a modified broken arpeggio strum (fig. 28, p. 40, Lesson 37, p 120), using the thumb, index, middle, and ring fingers. You can think of the last three strokes as a short Travis pattern. It should be played in a fast, flowing manner with very short, gentle strokes. Again, the use of picks depends on the toughness of the player's fingers.

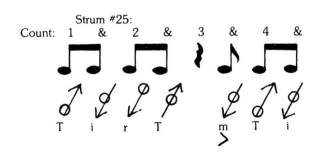

THIS TRAIN

Chords used: D, G, A7, &D7

This train is bound for glo-ry, this train._____

(Continue Strum)

This train is bound for glo-ry, this train._____ This train is

bound for glo-ry, don't car-ry nuth-in' but the right-eous and the ho - ly.

This train is bound for glo-ry this train._____

This train don't carry no gamblers, this train   no crap shooters, no midnight ramblers,
This train don't carry no gamblers, this train   This train is bound for glory, this train.
This train don't carry no gamblers,

        An interesting variation would be to substitute the blanking out stroke (Bl, p.91) for the "rest" on the 3rd beat. This would add a percussive effect to the syncopation.

        Practice songs for these strums include "Old Kimball," "Steal Away" and "Shoo Fly." Many pop favorites such as "Rhinestone Cowboy," "Let It Be, " "When You're Smiling," and "Have I Told You Lately That I Love You " are enhanced by these patterns.

LESSON 30: BLUES; Creating your own blues song

This next strum is also syncopated, but is built on the shuffle rhythm rather than the arpeggio pattern. It's similar to the Chicago style urban blues. It is really a variation of Strum #23c, (p.101) using pinches on the accented beats.

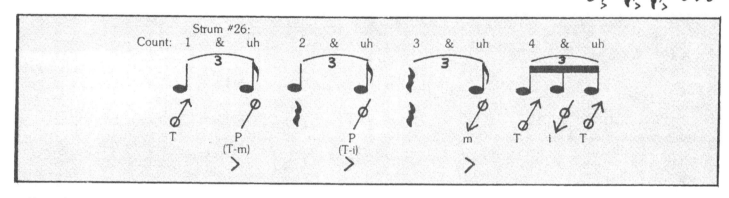

    Using this strum, or any other you've mastered or developed on your own, play the following 12 bar blues progression. You can even mix up the patterns, using a plain shuffle beat on one line, alternating with a syncopated or a triplet rhythm on the next. Play one complete strum per measure.

    As you play the progression over and over again, try to fit an original melody over the chords. Repeat this melody on the second line, and bring it to a conclusion on the last line.

    Do the same with the words. Take an everyday subject; something sad or something joyous; a problem or a frustration.

Ask a question or make a statement, repeating the first line, but changing the words and tune on the last line. The more emotion you put into your song, the better. Add other instruments, small percussion, clapping, and stomping. Make up several verses; use your imagination!

    I have put the chord designation in parenthesis next to each Roman Numeral for those who are not familiar with chord groupings written this way (see p.161).You can transpose to another key if you choose. I have also written a sample verse to get you started.

*See "Growth of Black Sound in America," by Carman Moore, 1980, Doubleday and Co., Inc., New York, N.Y.

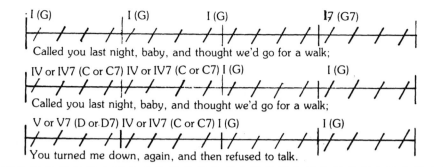

Called you last night, baby, and thought we'd go for a walk;

Called you last night, baby, and thought we'd go for a walk;

You turned me down, again, and then refused to talk.

LESSON 31: EARLY JAZZ AND DIXIELAND

Jazz has its roots in Black music. It is a synthesis of all the music heard during the slave period in New Orleans (French, Latin American, Spanish, West Indian) added to the hymns and popular tunes of English-speaking Americans and the blues. Combine this with a strong rhythmic heritage and you have a new sound. There were spirituals, work songs, and chants. But the key was improvisation both in words and music.

Out of this combination of sounds came the Dixieland Sound. This was early jazz, not the serious, sophisticated music it has become today.

To better understand these roots here are two songs used in a typical funeral procession in the Old South. The first is played on the way to the cemetery; sad and mournful, with obvious religious overtones ("Just A Closer Walk With Thee"). The second is an exciting rhythmic song played as the musicians returned from the burial ceremony ("When The Saints Go Marching In").

Both can be played with three finger variations of the triplet, shuffle and rocker strums used in the blues section.

The first strum is an offshoot of the simple arpeggio strum #11 (p. 40). However, it is played with a rocker beat and four identical finger patterns per measure. Here, again, the rhythm of the strum and the rhythm of the melody are different, making it more difficult but more interesting to master.

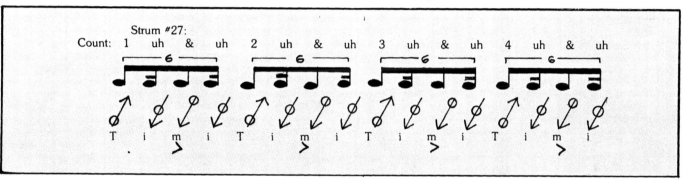

JUST A CLOSER WALK WITH THEE

Chords used: G, C, D7, & G7

Just a clo-ser walk with Thee,

Grant it, Je-sus, if you please_____ Dai - ly walk-in' close to

Thee Let it be, dear Lord, let it be.

Through the days of toil that's near,
If I fall dear Lord, who cares.
Who with me my burden share,
None but Thee, dear Lord, None but Thee.

When my feeble life is o'er,
Time for me will be no more.
Guide me gently, safely on,
To Thy shore, dear Lord, To Thy shore.

After you have played this slowly try it in double time for the real Dixieland flavor.

The second strum pattern has the same rocker beat, but the finger style is Travis. If the middle finger were omitted and the index finger continued to play in the middle octave, it would become, basically, double thumbing.

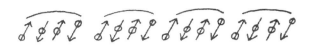

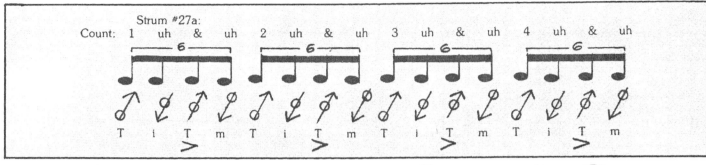

The next song requires only two finger patterns in each measure, so it would be written and counted as a basic shuffle rhythm with a blues accent.

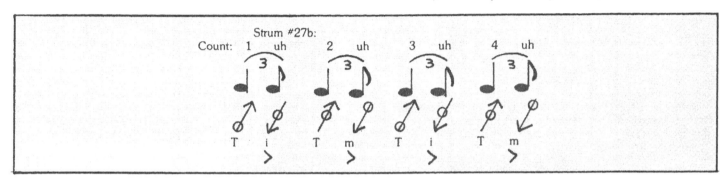

WHEN THE SAINTS GO MARCHING IN

Chords used: C, F, G7 & C7

2. And when the trumpet sounds a call.
   And when the trumpet sounds a call,
   Oh, Lord, I want to be in that number,
   When the saints go marching in.

See Hymns For Autoharp by Meg Peterson, Mel Bay Publications, p. 41. "What A Friend We Have In Jesus" and many other gospel songs can be played in Dixieland style.

The same strum can be used effectively on such jazz and blues favorites as "Didn't He Ramble", "St. Louis Blues", and "Basin Street Blues".

The next song can be played with the two previous patterns, or a variation of the Church Lick (Strum #6, p.27). When played very fast there is only time for the upstrokes. Naturally, the thumb plays an alternating bass.

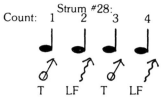

BILL BAILEY

(21 and 27 chord model)

Hughie Cannon

Chords used: D, G, A7, G7, D7, B7, & Em

*The G7 and D7 give a blues feeling to this old jazz tune. If you prefer, you can just use D-G-D in the last two measures.

This is an ideal song to play with a pattern already learned, which uses a pinch (P) and fast Travis picking. This strum (13b, p. 47) was played at a moderate tempo. Now, speed it up and see how different it sounds on "Bill Bailey." There are some tricky sections when you change in the middle of a strum pattern...so watch out!

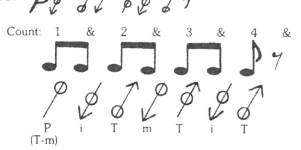

Count: 1 & 2 & 3 & 4 &

P i T m T i T
(T-m)

LESSON 32: RHYTHM AND BLUES

Rhythm and Blues began in the '30's in Black ghettoes around the country, and surfaced in the mid-1950's. This was the era of Chuck Berry, Bill Haley, Elvis Presley, and "Fats" Domino.

A combination of the rhythm and blues sound and country and western ushered in the early rock 'n roll characterized so well in the musical "Grease."

The following chord sequence used in the song "Those Magic Changes" in Grease, stems from the basic black male gospel quartet. This progression, which has been associated with popular music (e.g. "Blue Moon"; "Heart and Soul") over the years, is also found extensively in current church music: Gospel, Roman Catholic, and Protestant.

Count:	1	2	3	4	1	2	3	4
	C	/	Am	/	F	/	G	/

The same sequence can be played in the key of F like this:

	F	/	Dm	/	Bb	/	C	/

Try playing these eight bars with a combination shuffle and triplet strum, using steady strokes with the thumb in the lower octave.

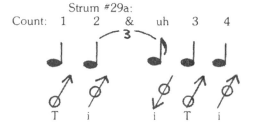

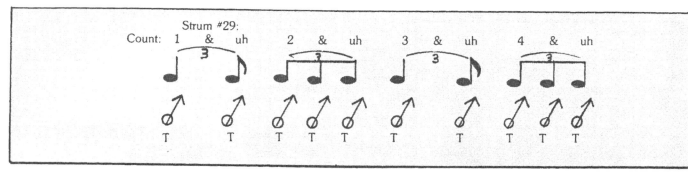

Strum #29:

Count: 1 & uh 2 & uh 3 & uh 4 & uh

T T T T T T T T T T

Change the chord sequence slightly and you have another popular progression used in such hits as "Happy Days" and "Tell Me You Love Me." In fact, several new songs use both sequences within the same composition.

Count:	1	2	3	4	1	2	3	4
	C	/	Am	/	Dm	/	G7	/
			OR:					
	F	/	Dm	/	Gm	/	C7	/

Now try the following tune which uses this chord sequence. Although it is an old folk song, it can be given a rhythm and blues feeling by using one of these next two strum patterns.

The triplet beat can be used, or altered to have the same feeling, but fewer strokes.

Strum #29a:

Count: 1 2 & uh 3 4

T i i T i

You will hear more of an early rock sound with this next strum, a steady driving beat with the thumb in the lower octave.

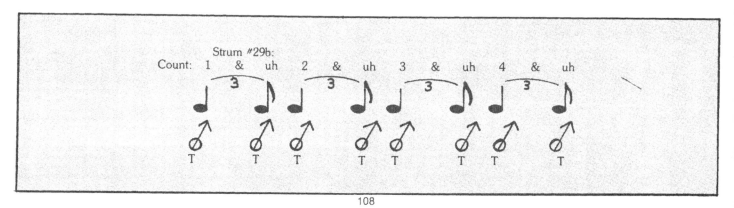

Strum #29b:

Count: 1 & uh 2 & uh 3 & uh 4 & uh

T T T T T T T T

108

I LOVE THE MOUNTAINS

Chords used: F, Dm, Gm, & C7

I love the moun - tains, I love the roll - ing hills,

(Continue Strum)

I love the flow - ers, I love the daf - fo - dils,

I love the fire - side When all the lights are low. Boom-dee-ah - da,

(After 2nd time, go to Coda) D.S.*

Coda*

boom-dee-ah - da, Boom-dee-ah - da, boom-dee-ah - da boom.

* For explanation of D.S. and Coda see p. 11

Another rhythmic pattern widely used in the '50's was made popular by Bo Diddley. It is a two bar strum played with the Loose Fist (LF) in the middle octave.

Strum #30:

Count: 1   2 & 3 & 4 | 1 2 3 4

As you practice repeat the phrase: um chuka chuka chuk (um) chuk chuk. The "um" in parenthesis must be felt, even 'though it signifies a rest.

LF LF LF LF LF LF   LF LF

Chords used: D, G, & A7   Now apply this strum to a 1950's favorite: **STAGOLEE**

1. Stag - o - lee was an aw - ful man Ev - 'ry - bod - y knows,

Spent two hun - dred dol - lars to buy a suit of clothes; He was a

(Continue Strum)

bad man   mean old Stag - o - lee.

109

LESSON 33: ROCK

There are many kinds of rock music, from the early rock 'n 'roll that is having a revival, to hard rock, acid rock, soft rock, country rock, and folk rock. The last three are best suited to the Autoharp.

One accompaniment is characterized by the blues pattern already learned (Strum #22); 4/4 time in triplets. A more typical rock sound, however, is a straight 8 beats to the measure played very rhythmically and evenly. This next strum uses this pattern on an old spiritual. Play using the loose fist (LF) for the upstroke and the thumbnail for the downstroke (See Fig. 50). Play in the middle octave.

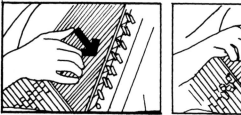

Fig. 50 Rock strum

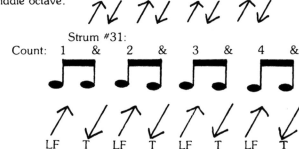

Strum #31:
Count: 1 & 2 & 3 & 4 &

LF T LF T LF T LF T

JOSHUA FIT THE BATTLE OF JERICHO

Chords used: Dm, Gm, & A7

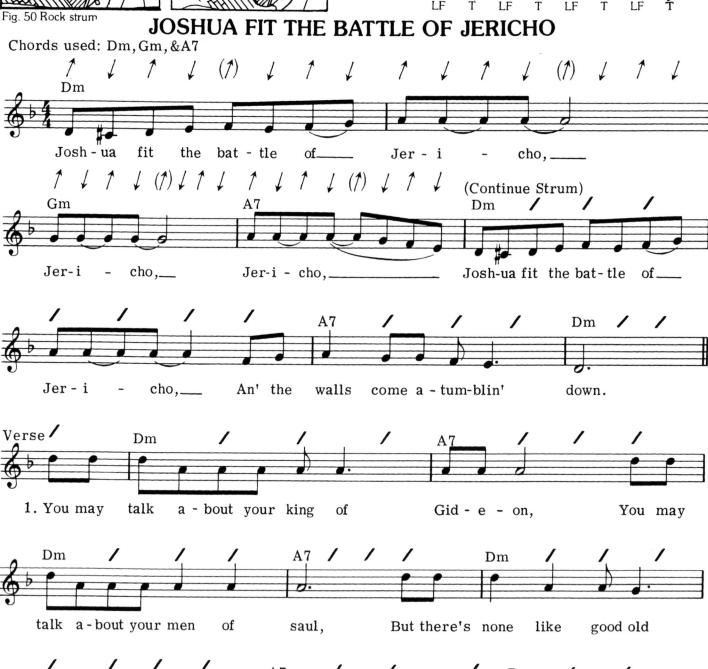

Josh-ua fit the bat-tle of___ Jer-i - cho,___

Jer-i - cho,___ Jer-i - cho,_____ Josh-ua fit the bat-tle of___

(Continue Strum)

Jer - i - cho,___ An' the walls come a - tum-blin' down.

Verse

1. You may talk a - bout your king of Gid - e - on, You may

talk a - bout your men of saul, But there's none like good old

Josh-u - a At the bat-tle of Jer-i - cho.___

2. Right up to the wall of Jericho
He marched with spear in hand;
"Now go blow those rams horn,"
Joshua cried,
" 'Cause the battle is in my hand!"

3. Then Joshua had the people blow
On the trumpets with mighty sound,
'An they blew so awful loud and long
That the walls come tumblin' down!

Now try a variation of this pattern, remaining silent on the 3rd beat as in the syncopated calypso strum #14 (p.81). This Latin American influence is evident in many rock pieces.

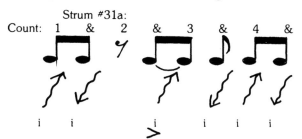

After you have played these two strums, *double the tempo* (speed) and try the next six strums, all variations on the straight eight beat pattern. In fact, if you have several Autoharps you can make a rock ensemble, each player choosing his favorite pattern while others sing along.

Here is another syncopated strum, except the "rest" (𝄾) is on the 2nd instead of the 3rd beat. You'll recognize it as the sort of pattern used by an electric rhythm guitar in a rock group.

Notice how important the accent is to the feeling of the music.

Strum #31a:

Count: 1 & 2 & 3 & 4 &

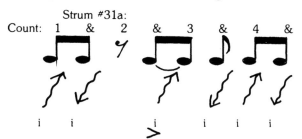

The very fast arpeggiando strokes are done with the index finger in the two higher octaves. This strum can also be done very effectively using the blank (Bl) stroke on the 2nd and 3rd beats only (p.91). When the "rest" on the 2nd beat is muffled it stops the vibrating strings suddenly and accentuates the syncopation. Then stroke on the "and 3" count while the strings are dampened. The last three strokes are played in the regular way.

This next pattern is similar to the scratch style in strum #8c (p.35) and is typical of those played by an acoustic guitar. For an authentic sound use the thumb and nail of the index finger without picks.

Strum #31b:

Count: 1 2 & 3 & 4 &

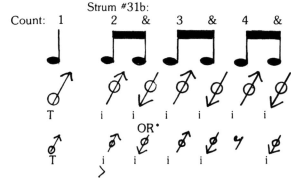

*This alternative pattern is syncopated on the 4th beat with a slight accent on the 2nd.

The next strum has the same rhythm as the previous one, but is in classical guitar style, using the pinch (P) and a Travis pattern similar to strum #13b (p.47). It can be done with or without picks.

Strum #31c:

Count: 1 2 & 3 & 4 &

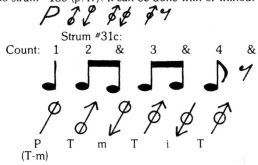

The following two patterns are two measure strums which fill in as a heavy bass line. Their accents and rhythm are complimentary and can be used very successfully together, along with the three previous strums.

In this one the arpeggiando strokes are heavy, and cover the two lower octaves.

Strum #32:

Count: 1 & 2 & 3 & 4 & | 1 2 3 4

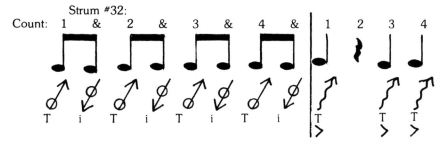

This strum has a slightly different syncopation, the accent in the first measure, and a straight eight beat Travis pattern (strum #13a, p.46) in the second.

Strum #32a:

Count: 1 2 3 4 & | 1 & 2 & 3 & 4 &

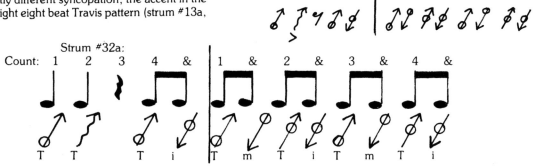

To complete your rock ensemble play this final strum, using an adaptation of a typical Beatles drum beat. Notice the strong accents on 2 and 4, a forerunner of the reggae sound.

Take any favorite spiritual or pop ballad in 4/4 time and see how you can get the rock feeling by accompanying it with these fast strums. For practice songs try, "Down By The Riverside" (p.33), "Do, Lord" (p.30), "Oh, Them Golden Slippers" (p.49), "Will The Circle Be Unbroken", and "Let My Little Light Shine" (p148)

Strum #33:

Count: 1 2 3 & 4

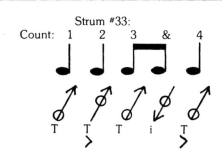

LESSON 34: ROCK;
Tapping Stroke

Try the next few rock patterns on your favorite current hit tunes. The first one is syncopated and employs a gentle, bouncing tap with the fingertips, spanning most of the strings.

Picks *must* be used on all fingers. The ends of the finger make contact with the strings in a crisp, rapid motion. For clarity of tone use an amplified Autoharp.

Fig.51 Tapping

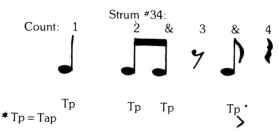

This same stroke is effective on many melody songs. Each melody chord is tapped rather than strummed or pinched. (See "Battle Hymn of the Republic," p152).

Strum #34:

Count: 1   2 & 3 & 4

* Tp = Tap   Tp   Tp Tp   Tp

·A Rasgueado (R, p.83) can be substituted for this final tap, if preferred.

Any of the rock strums from the previous lesson could also be applied to this song very effectively.

HEAV'N HEAV'N
(All God's Chillun)

Chords used: G, C&D7

I got a robe, You got a robe, All God's chil-lun got a robe.

When I get to heav-en gon-na put on my robe, I'm gon-na shout all o-ver God's heav-en_____ Heav-en,_____ Heav-en,_____

Ev'-ry-bod-y talk-in' 'bout Heav'n ain't go-in' there, heav-en,_____

Heav-en,_____ Gon-na shout all o-ver God's Heav'n._____

112

On the next variation tap the strings with the chord bar up on the 1st half of the count of 2, and press the chord bar down on the 2nd half. This gives the typical "ah-um" effect of *hammerin' on*, Ⓗ but is done with a tap rather than a pinch, thumb, or finger stroke.

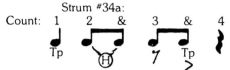

A further variation would substitute a slap (SI) Fig. 42, (p. 84) for a tap, or use a combination of slaps and taps thoughout the pattern.

Strum #34a:

Count: 1   2   &   3   &   4

Still another variation would be to tap the strings with the chord bar up on the 2nd half of the 2nd beat, depressing the chord on the count of 3. The accent would be shifted to the Ⓗ and a tap on the count of 3 would follow immediately.

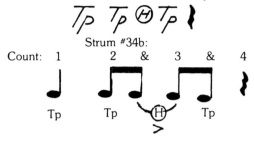

Strum #34b:

Count: 1   2   &   3   &   4

Tp   Tp   Ⓗ   Tp

LESSON 35: ROCK;
Advanced Strums

The next pattern, a two bar strum is especially suited to folk rock. There are no octave designations since it is effective in both the lower and middle, or the middle and higher octaves. The small pinches can also be done with the thumb and index finger, although in a rapid strum like this most players find them more easily executed with the thumb and middle finger.

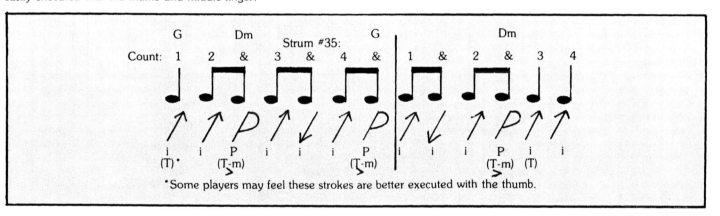

Strum #35:

Count: 1 2 & 3 & 4 & | 1 & 2 & 3 4

    i   i   P   i   i   i   P | i   i   i   P   i   i
   (T)*   (T-m)   (T-m) | (T-m) (T)

*Some players may feel these strokes are better executed with the thumb.

INSTRUCTION CASSETTE
TUNING CASSETTE

To use with this book and learn faster!

Many people find it much easier, faster, and more effective to learn a musical instrument with the aid of a related tape. To help these folks, Meg Peterson has prepared a 70-minute cassette tape which takes you step by step thru each of the lessons and lets you hear those sounds she writes about in the book. She demonstrates all those licks and strums. You'll hear them precisely as they should sound. Then you can copy them correctly. This cassette is an invaluable aid to the beginner and more advanced student as well.

Equally important is the tuning of your instrument. An out-of-tune instrument can mislead you as you learn. Meg's tuning cassette will show you how to tune easily, quickly, and stay that way. The notes are

true string sounds, not electronic simulations. One side is the method for the non-musician or beginner. On the other side is a faster method for the musician or more experienced player. Helpful hints for instrument care and the changing of strings for both Autoharp and Chromaharp are included. No better tuning aid has even been developed!

To get the feel of the rhythm use the G and Dm chord changes as they appear over the strum pattern. Practice going from one octave to another, and notice what an interesting melody you can create by just repeating the strum.

After you have mastered the finger technique use it on this old song.

DRILL, YE TARRIERS, DRILL

Chords Used: Am, E7, C, F, & G

Now, our new foreman was Jim McCann,
By God, he was a blame mean man,
Last week a premature blast went off,
And a mile in the air went Big Jim Goff,
And drill, ye tarriers, drill.

The next time payday come around,
Jim Goff a dollar short was found.
When he asked, "What for?" came this reply,
"You're docked for the time you was up in the sky"...

Rock music is full of characteristic interludes and progressions. They can introduce a ballad, serve as a bridge between two verses, or provide an interesting ending. Here is one of those interludes using an arpeggiando stroke over all three octaves, and some fast syncopation. Finger designations are provided under the long brush (Br) strokes, since they had only been done with the thumb, previously (p. 32). This is a 4 bar exercise.

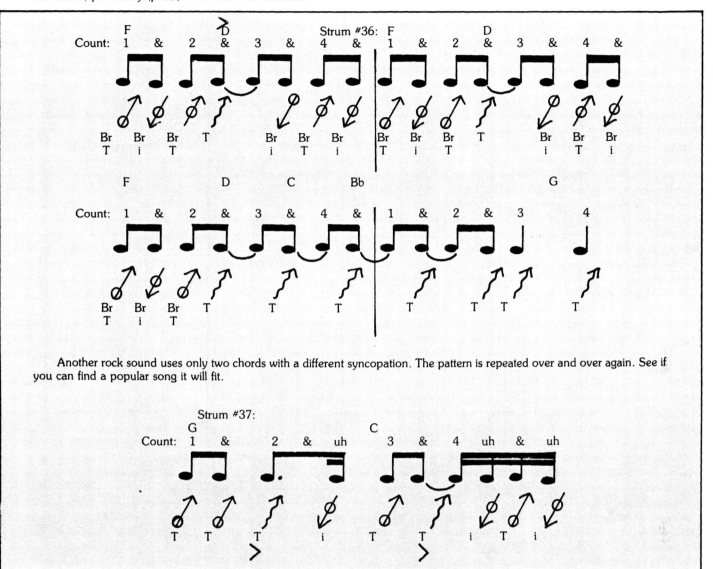

Another rock sound uses only two chords with a different syncopation. The pattern is repeated over and over again. See if you can find a popular song it will fit.

The next ballad makes a good transition from a steady folk-rock strum to the flowing arpeggio strums in Lesson 36.

First, play the song using this slow even pattern:

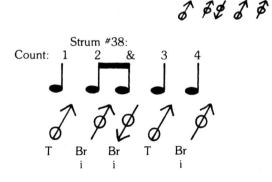

A loose fist (LF) or thumb can be used throughout the piece, if preferred. The next tune is similar to Elvis Presley's big hit "Love Me Tender."

AURA LEE
(21 and 27 chord model)

W.W. Fosdick
and
George R. Poulton

Chords used: G, D7, A7, E7, B7, &Em

As the black-bird in the spring, 'neath the wil-low tree_____ Sat and piped I heard him sing, Sing of Au-ra Lee, Au-ra Lee, Au-ra Lee, Maid of gold-en hair, Sun-shine came a-long with thee, And swal-lows in the air.

In thy blush the rose was born;	Aura Lee, the bird may flee,
Music when you spake.	The willow's golden hair.
Through thine azure eyes the moon	Swing through winter fitfully,
Sparkling seemed to break.	On the stormy air.
Aura Lee, Aura Lee,	Yet if thy blue eyes I see,
Birds of crimson wing	Gloom will soon depart.
Never song have sung to me	For to me, sweet Aura Lee
As in that bright, sweet spring.	Is sunshine through the heart.

When the mistletoe was green
'Midst the winter's snows,
Sunshine in thy face was seen,
Kissing lips of rose.
   Aura Lee, Aura Lee,
   Take my golden ring.
   Love and light return with thee,
   And swallows with the spring.

LESSON 36: ADVANCED ARPEGGIO STRUMS; TRIPLET ARPEGGIO IN 4/4

You have already been introduced to simple arpeggio strums in lesson 9 (p. 38). These strums use three to five fingers to pluck a "broken chord," playing the notes consecutively, one string at a time, instead of stroking several strings in any of the designated octaves. Do not try to pick single strings, just pluck as few strings as possible in a gentle, flowing manner. Use picks on all fingers to insure uniformity of sound.

Try playing "Aura Lee" again, using a variation of strum #11 (p.40) in 4/4 time. This pattern is in the shape of a curve, moving upward over the strings and back down again.

Fig. 52: Triplet arpeggio strum

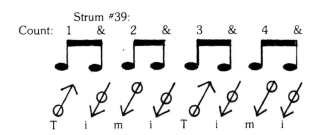

Now add the ring finger and change to triplet timing. Pluck three single strings, one after the other, in each beat, counting as you practice:

one - da - da, two - da - da, three - da - da, four - da - da, or
one - and - uh, two - and - uh, three - and - uh, four - and - uh, or
one - trip - let, two - trip - let, three - trip - let, four - trip - let.

This makes twelve short strokes per measure rather than eight, as in the previous strum. Remember, even 'though the octave designation is the same for some adjoining strokes, pluck each time in a slightly different area.

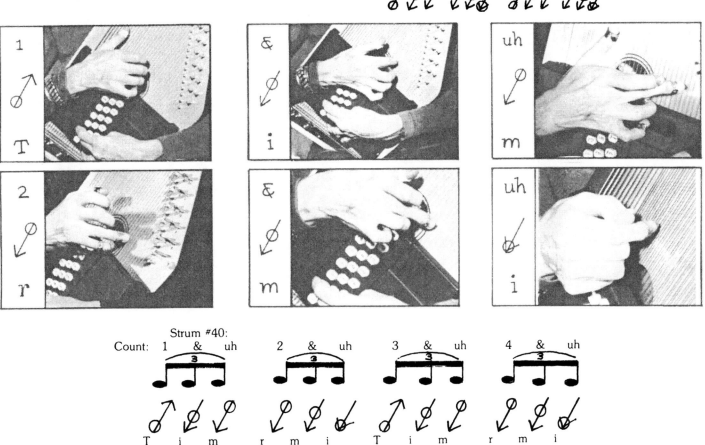

AURA LEE
(21 and 27 chord model)

Chords used: G, D7, A7, E7, B7, & Em

As you play "Aura Lee" alternate the thumb strokes, playing the first one on the lowest string of the lower octave and the second one a few strings higher.

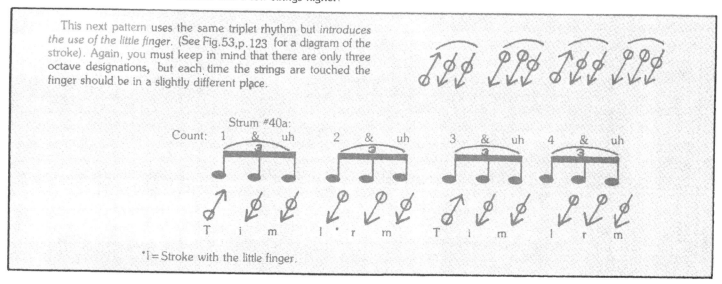

This next pattern uses the same triplet rhythm but *introduces the use of the little finger.* (See Fig.53,p.123 for a diagram of the stroke). Again, you must keep in mind that there are only three octave designations, but each time the strings are touched the finger should be in a slightly different place.

Strum #40a:
Count: 1 & uh 2 & uh 3 & uh 4 & uh

T i m l·r m T i m l r m

*l = Stroke with the little finger.

NOW THE DAY IS OVER

Chords used: C, G, D7, E7, G7, & Am

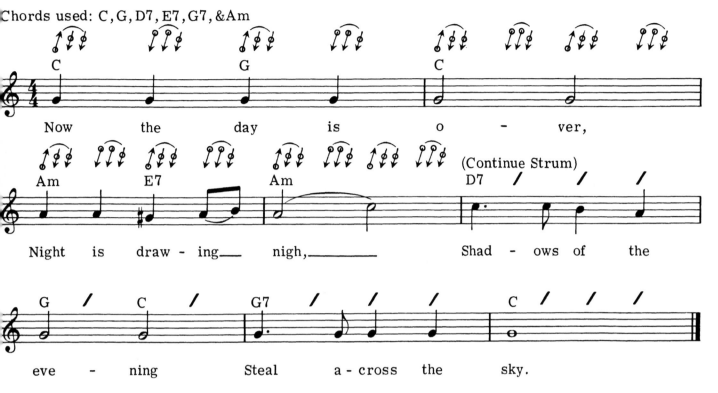

Now   the   day   is   o - ver,

Night is draw - ing___ nigh,_____   Shad - ows of the

eve - ning   Steal   a - cross the   sky.

2. Jesus give the weary
   Calm and sweet repose
   With the tend' rest blessing
   May our eyelids close.

3. When the morning wakens,
   Then may we arise
   Pure and fresh and sinless,
   In Thy holy eyes.

Some good practice songs using the triplet arpeggio strum in 4/4 time are "Lonesome Road" (p. 21), "Shenandoah" (p. 27), and "Red River Valley" (p. 19).

TRIPLET ARPEGGIO IN 3/4

The triplet arpeggio can be played in 3/4 time using the following pattern. Notice that the thumb has only one short upstroke on the first beat, followed by tiny downstroke plucks with the other four fingers. The strum starts in the lower octave and gradually works its way to the higher.

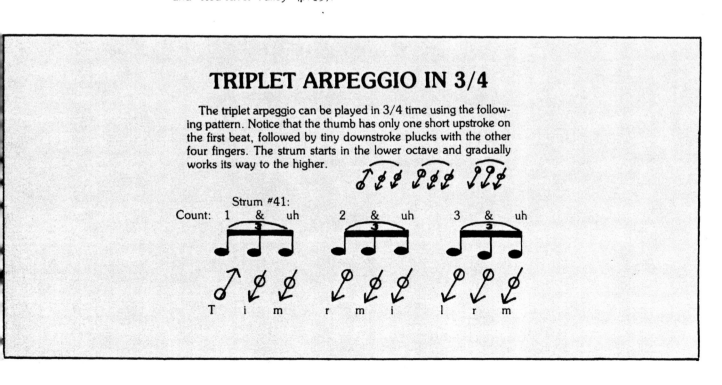

See how interesting the pattern sounds on this familiar old hymn.

AMAZING GRACE

Chords used: F, B♭, C7, & Dm

A - mas - ing____ Grace, how sweet the

(Continue Strum)

sound, that____ saved a____ wretch like__ me____

I____ once was____ lost, But__ now I'm

found, was__ blind but__ now I see.____

Other practice songs for the 3/4 triplet arpeggio strum are "Down In The Valley" (p. 38), "The Unquiet Grave," and "Streets of Laredo" (p. 20).

LESSON 37: ADVANCED ARPEGGIO STRUMS; BROKEN ARPEGGIO PATTERNS IN 4/4

First play a straight 4/4 arpeggio with an alternating bass. The fingers move in an upward pattern with the thumb hitting a higher section of the lower octave on the 3rd beat.

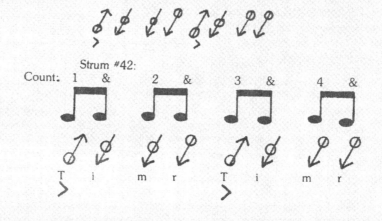

Strum #42:

Count: 1 & 2 & 3 & 4 &

T i m r T i m r

120

HAND ME DOWN MY WALKING CANE

Chords used: D, G, &A7

Hand me down my walk-ing cane____

____ Hand me down my walk-ing

(Continue Strum)

cane____ Hand me down my walk-ing

cane, I'm gon-na leave on the mid-night train, all my

sins been tak-en a-way tak-en a-way____

Verse:

I got drunk, and I got in jail
I got drunk, and I got in jail
I got drunk, and I got in jail
Had no one to go my bail
All my sins been taken away, taken away
Chorus

Now, change this straight pattern to a broken arpeggio. This means, of course, that the notes of the chord are not plucked in order and the player skips around in different octaves. The gentle playing style is the same, however.

In this variation the middle and ring finger are alternating with the index finger. The octave designations depend on the player, since the entire pattern can be moved to the middle and higher octaves, if preferred. Try this one without picks.

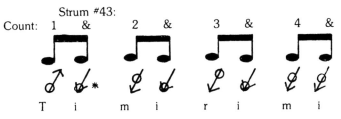

*The index finger plucks a higher string in the lower octave on each downstroke.

BLACK IS THE COLOR (OF MY TRUE LOVE'S HAIR)

American Mountain Song

Chords used: Dm, C, Am, Dm, & Gm

Black, black black is the col - or of my

true love's hair, Her lips_____ are some-thing

won - drous fair, Her____ eyes so____ pure, and the

dain - ti -est hands, I love_____ the ground on which she stands.

The next strum adds the little finger. The index finger now plucks a little higher, in the first few strings of the middle octave.

Strum #43a:

Count: 1 & 2 & 3 & 4 &
T i m i r i l i

LET US BREAK BREAD TOGETHER

Chords used: C, F, G7, A7, G, Am, Dm, & (Em)

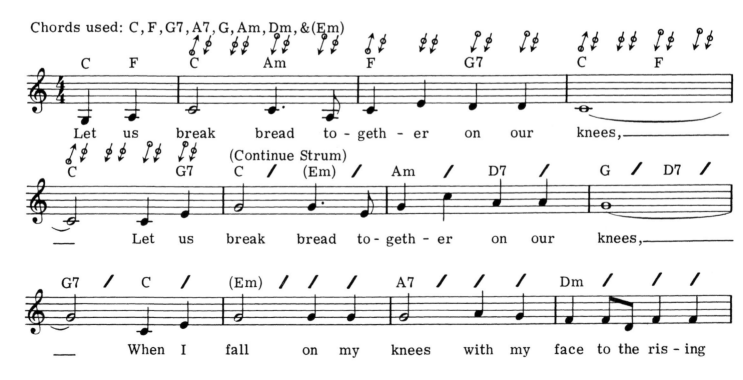

Let us break bread to - geth - er on our knees,_____

Let us break bread to - geth - er on our knees,_____

When I fall on my knees with my face to the ris - ing

122

sun,   Oh   Lord,   have   mer - cy   on   me _____

Try another broken arpeggio pattern on the same song. Then make up some strums of your own, using all five fingers. You can see how many possible combinations there are.

Strum #43b:

Count: 1 &   2 &   3 &   4 &

T i   m r   m r   m i

Another variation which also fits the three previous songs begins as a broken arpeggio on the first 2 beats and leads into a straight backward arpeggio on the last 2 beats. Remember that each finger plucks a different string even though the octave designations are often the same.

Fig. 53: Straight backward arpeggio Strum #43c

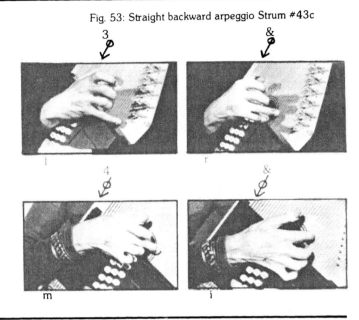

Strum #43c:

Count: 1 &   2 &   3 &   4 &

T i   m i   l r   m i

Some good practice songs using straight and broken arpeggio strums in 4/4 time are "Long, Long Ago" (p. 45), "I Know Where I'm Goin'" (p150), "Go Tell Aunt Rhody" (p. 77), and "Wayfaring Stranger" (p. 26).

LESSON 38: ADVANCED ARPEGGIO STRUMS; BROKEN ARPEGGIO PATTERNS IN 3/4

To learn more advanced 3/4 arpeggio strumming on the Autoharp, start by varying simple strum #11 (p. 40). Add the ring finger to the regular strum.

Strum #44:

Count: 1 &   2 &   3 &

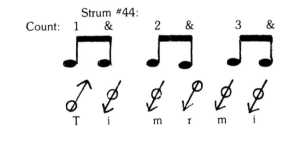

T i   m r   m i

Now turn this into a simple straight arpeggio strum which moves up the strings with the help of an alternating bass. Start the second thumb stroke in the upper part of the lower octave. Notice that the accents on the alternating bass pattern give a feeling of syncopation to the rhythm.

Strum #44a:

Count: 1 &   2 &   3 &

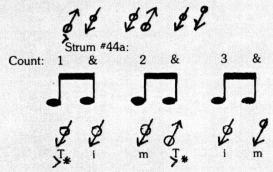

T i   m T   i m

Try both strums on the next old folk song.

SCARBOROUGH FAIR

Chords used: Am, G, C, D, & F

Are you go-ing to Scar-bor-ough Fair?

(Continue Strum)

Pars-ley sage, rose-mar-y and thyme. Re-mem-ber me to one who lives there, For once she was a true love of mine.

If you reverse the straight arpeggio and play descending notes, starting with the little finger in the higher octave, you have this pattern.

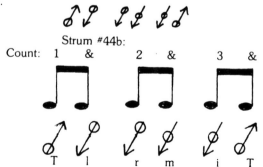

Strum #44b:

Count: 1 & 2 & 3 &

T l r m i T

With or without picks this harp-like strum lends itself to the next popular old English ballad.

GREENSLEEVES

Two final variations of 3/4 patterns use broken arpeggio strums. The first one is similar to Strum #43.

The second is used by many folk rock guitarists to accompany their songs.

Try them both on this old romantic ballad.

TELL ME WHY

Chords used: G, C, D7, A7, G7, &E7

Other songs which lend themselves to these 3/4 arpeggio strums are "Green Grow The Lilacs," "My Bonnie" (p. 39), "The Man On The Flying Trapeze," and "Annie's Song."

126

LESSON 39: ADVANCED ARPEGGIO STRUMS; COMBINATION PATTERNS WITH DOUBLE STOPS

The arpeggio strum can be combined with many forms of finger picking, one of which is double stops. A double stop in Autoharp terminology means that two or more fingers pluck the strings simultaneously, sounding different intervals of the depressed chord. Each finger plucks only one string, if possible. These are not pinches nor up or downstrokes. Therefore, no arrows are used. Octave designations are given only if two fingers play in one particular octave. When three fingers are used it is understood that one usually plucks in the adjoining octave, since three to four inches of string area are covered.

Play the next pattern to accompany "Tell Me Why," learned in the previous lesson. It's good to get used to playing without picks, since it gives a more pleasant, harp-like sound. Leave the picks off for longer periods each time you practice, until your fingers have formed callouses.

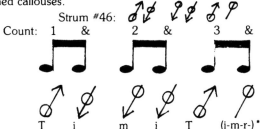

*(t-m-r) = Pluck three strings simultaneously with the index, middle, and ring finger.

BEAUTIFUL DREAMER

Stephen Foster

Chords used: C, F, G7, D7, E7, Am, & Dm

127

song,_____ List while I woo

thee with soft mel - o - dy_____

Gone are the cares of life's bu - sy

throng,_____ Beau - ti - ful dream - er a -

wake un - to me_____ Beau - ti - ful

dream - er, a - wake un - to me._____

Fig. 54: Three finger double stop

When you play this same pattern in 4/4 time it is much slower.

As you practice repeat the words:

boom - a - chick - a - boom - chick

Strum #47:

Count: 1 & 2 & 3 4

T i m i T (i-m-r)

See how effective the pattern is on this old English folk song.

THE FOGGY, FOGGY DEW

Chords used: G, C, D7, & Am

When I was a bach - 'lor I lived by my-self, I

worked at the weav - er's trade,___ And the on-ly, on-ly thing I

did that was wrong was to woo a fair young maid. I wooed her in the

win - ter - time, And in the sum-mer too, And the on-ly, on-ly thing I

did that was wrong was to keep her from the fog - gy, fog - gy dew.

One night she knelt close by my side
As I lay fast asleep.
She threw her arms around my neck,
And then began to weep.
She wept, she cried, she tore her hair,
Ah me, what could I do?
So all night long I held her in my arms
Just to keep her from the foggy, foggy dew.

Oh, I am a bachelor, I live with my son,
We work at the weaver's trade.
And every single time I look into his eyes
He reminds me of the fair young maid.
He reminds me of the winter time,
And of the summer too.
And the many, many times I held her in my arms
Just to keep her from the foggy, foggy dew.

Now, reverse the pattern and play the double stop on the 2nd instead of the 4th beat.

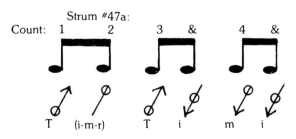

The count now becomes:
boom - chick
boom - a - chick - a

Play "Foggy, Foggy Dew" again—this time without picks.

The next strum is a variation of simple arpeggio strum #11 (p. 40).

For this double stop only two strings are sounded at once, rather than three (as in the previous pattern). Be sure to alternate the pitch of the thumb stroke.

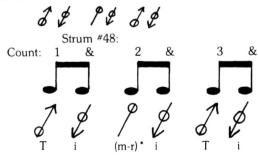

*(m-r) = Pluck two strings simultaneously with the middle and ring finger.

Play this pattern on one of the rare 3/4 time blues melodies.

HOUSE OF THE RISING SUN

Chords used: Am, C, D7, F, (F7), E7, &Dm

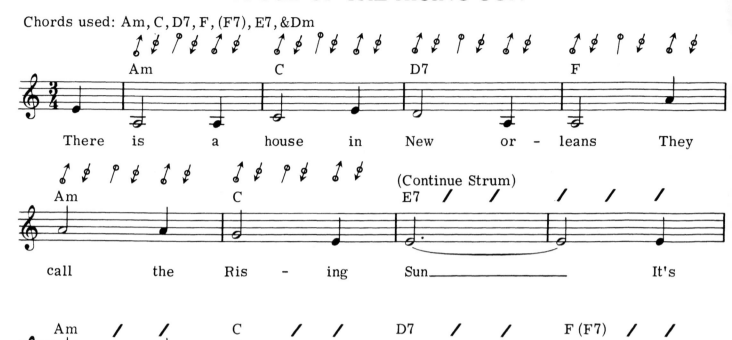

There is a house in New or-leans They call the Ris - ing Sun_____ It's been the ru-in of man-y poor gals, and me, dear God,___ I'm___ one_____

As you become more familiar with playing double stops add another on the 3rd beat to create this next variation.

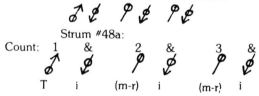

Strum #48a:
Count: 1 & 2 & 3 &
T i (m-r) i (m-r) i

Now experiment on the following practice songs: "Let Us Break Bread Together" (p122), "Drunken Sailor" (p.23), "Bury Me Not On The Lone Prairie" (p.70), and "Old Abram Brown."

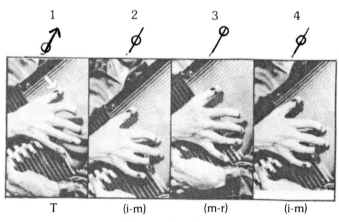

1 2 3 4

T (i-m) (m-r) (i-m)

Fig. 55: Lute Strum

LESSON 40: LUTE STRUM

This slow pattern uses a thumb stroke in the lower octave followed by three double stops. This time two of the double stops are played by the index and middle finger and one by the middle and ring finger. Remember, the hand is relaxed and slightly curved and the two fingers gently pluck the strings at the same time about an inch apart. There is a slight downward motion as the fingers brush the strings. Do not grab or pinch.

This strum attempts to imitate the lyric quality of the old English lute players. Therefore, Elizabethan tunes, Renaissance ballads, and madrigals can be played on the Autoharp with this style of plucking. No picks are used.

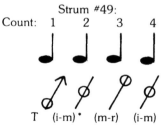

Strum #49:
Count: 1 2 3 4

T (i-m)* (m-r) (i-m)

*(i-m) = Pluck two strings simultaneously with the index and middle finger.

NOBODY KNOWS THE TROUBLE I'VE SEEN

To vary this strum play the entire pattern in the lower and middle octave. You can also slow the piece down so two complete patterns can be played in every measure.

Another variation doubles the speed of the strum and increases the number of double stops.

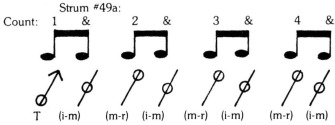

See how well this fits the following old Scottish melody.

ANNIE LAURIE

Chords used: C, F, G7, G, D7, Am, E7, & Dm

Max - wel - ton's braes are bon - nie, where

ear - ly fa's the___ dew, And it's there that An - nie

Lau-rie Gave me her prom - ise true. Gave

me her prom - ise true, which ne'er for - got will

be. And for bon - nie An - nie___

Lau - rie___ I'd___ lay___ me doon and dee

This is a very rich arrangement, harmonically, but those who find the middle section a little high for comfortable singing can move an octave lower during that section, or use the transposition chart (p.164), and change to the lower key of A.

This time speed up the song and use a variation of strum #49, adding a thumb stroke in place of a double stop on the 3rd beat. Be sure your thumb strokes alternate from lower to higher.

This same pattern can be written in 2/4 time (see p. 8 for an explanation of timing) and counted "1 & 2 &." Try it on this old Elizabethan round, being sure to continue the alternating bass (thumb) stroke.

Notice how the chord sequence is identical in each line, as is true of all rounds. This is an especially rich arrangement with many chord changes. Once you learn the progression you will see that each chord change falls on the thumb stroke; two per measure.

COME FOLLOW
(21 & 27 chord model)

John Hilton

Chords used: Bb, Eb, F7, Gm, Dm, &Cm

Come fol - low, fol - low, fol - low, fol - low, fol - low,

fol - low me. Whi-ther shall I fol - low, fol - low, fol - low,

Whi-ther shall I fol - low, fol - low, thee? To the green - wood,

to the green - wood, to the green-wood, fol - low, me.

Practice songs for these strums in 4/4 time, include "Loch Lomond" (p.151), "John Peel", "Go Down, Moses", "Careless Love" (p.72), "Danny Boy", and "Joy To The World".

A final example of the lute strum is this next 3/4 pattern.

Strum #50:

Count: 1 2 3

T (i-m) (m-r)

BELIEVE ME IF ALL THOSE ENDEARING YOUNG CHARMS

Chords used: C, F, G7, Dm, E7, C7, &D7

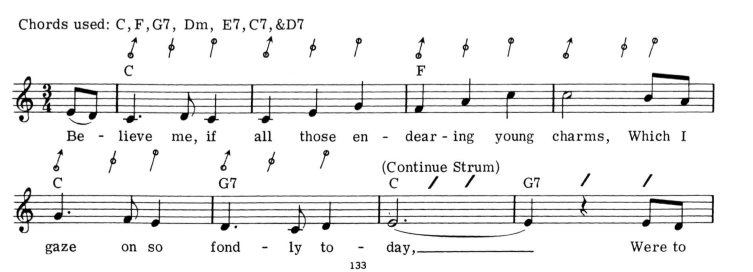

Be - lieve me, if all those en - dear - ing young charms, Which I

gaze on so fond - ly to - day, _____ Were to

change by to-mor-row and fleet in my arms, Like____

fair-y gifts fad-ing a-way,_____ Thou would

still be a-dored, As this mo-ment thou art, Let thy

love-li-ness fade as it will,_____ And a-

round the dear ru-in each wish of my heart, Would en-

twine it-self ver-dant-ly still._____

You can create numerous variations of this simple pattern and try them on such old familiar songs as "Randall, My Son," "Beautiful Dreamer" (p127), "Billy Barlow," "Lord Lovel," and "On Top of Old Smoky" (p.20). Any song with a simple tune, a haunting, mysterious quality, and a story to tell fits right in with the feeling of the lute strum.

LESSON 41: SYNCOPATED ARPEGGIO STRUMS:

This next strum is counted the same as calypso strum #14 (p.81). It combines a broken arpeggio roll on the first four strokes with a partial Travis pattern on the last 3 strokes. Be sure to observe the accents, and remain silent on the 3rd beat.

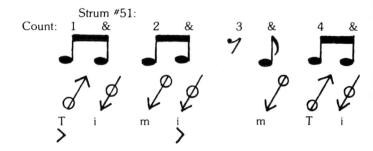

Since this is a calypso beat, play a typical calypso song.

LINSTEAD MARKET

Chords used: D, G, &A7

He prom-ised to meet___ me at Lin - stead Mar - ket, take me out___ to a show. He prom-ised to meet___ me at Lin - stead Mar - ket, take me out___ to a show.

Chorus:

I tell you, Oh what a night, what a night, oh what a Sat - ur-day night.(I tell___ a you) Oh what a night, what a night,___ Oh what a Sat - ur - day night!

2. I waited and waited at Linstead Market,
   Not a sign of my Joe.

3. Everybody coming to Linstead Market,
   Everybody but Joe.

4. Then I got a letter to Linstead Market,
   Explaining everything then.

5. Sorry can't meet you at Linstead
         Market,
   I just got married today.

Now, reverse the pattern, playing two backward arpeggios interrupted by a rest on the 3rd beat. Keep the identical time, but leave off the accents. This is a good strum for many traditional gospel and folk songs, for it provides a syncopated accompaniment to contrast with the even rhythm of the melody.

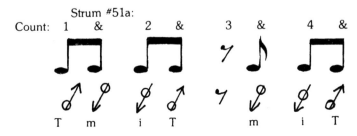

The chord changes are few, but fitting the strum into the melody is tricky in this next old gospel song. Four times you must change chords on the "rest" in the strum pattern, and sound the harmony on the up-beat. Press hard on that 3rd beat change to emphasize the "rest."

STANDIN' IN THE NEED OF PRAYER

Chords used: C, F, G7, D7, E7, C7, & Am

It's me,   it's   me, oh Lord,   Stand-in' in the need of   pray'r   It's

me,   it's   me,   oh Lord,   stand-in' in the need   of   pray'r.

1. Ain't my   broth-er   or   my   sis - ter   but   it's   me,   oh   Lord

stand-in' in   the need of   pray'r,   Ain't my broth-er or my sis-ter but it's

me,   oh   Lord,   stand-in' in   the need   of   pray'r.

2. Ain't my father or my mother, but it's me, oh Lord...

3. Ain't the preacher or the deacon, but it's me, oh Lord...

4. Ain't my neighbor or a stranger, but it's me, oh Lord...

You can experiment with other backward arpeggios. Try starting on the second stroke with the little finger and picking up the
beat after the "rest" with the ring finger. You could call this a backward broken arpeggio.

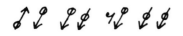

Strum #51b:

Play this pattern on the previous song and see if it doesn't flow
more naturally with only one thumb stroke and a more relaxed
position for the remaining fingers.

COMBINING SYNCOPATION AND HAMMERIN' ON

A final variation of strum #51 uses *hammerin' on* (H) in place of the "rest" on the 3rd beat. You have already been introduced to this technique in lesson 17 (p.73).

Count: one - and - two - and - three - uh - and - four - and.

Use a gentle brush with the thumb on the open strings of the lower octave on the "three" and immediately depress the chord bar on the "uh." This gives the "ah - um" effect. The last three strokes continue with the same broken arpeggio figure as the first four strokes.

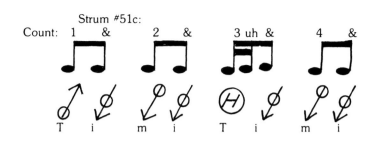

BIG ROCK CANDY MOUNTAIN

Chords used: C, F, & G7

On a sum-mer's day in the month of May, A___ bur-ly bum came

hik-ing. Down a shad-y lane, through the sug-ar cane, He was

look-ing for his lik-ing. As he strolled a-long he

sang this song, of the land of milk and hon-ey, Where a

bum can stay for___ man-y a day, And he won't need an-y

Chorus

mon-ey. Oh, the buzz-in' of the bees in the cig-a-rette trees, The

so-da wa-ter foun-tain, By the lem-on-ade springs where the

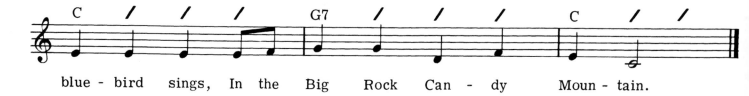

blue - bird sings, In the Big Rock Can - dy Moun - tain.

Practice songs for these four strums can include any of the calypso songs in this book, many of John Denver's hits such as "Sunshine On My Shoulder," and folk songs such as "Tom Dooley," "Lonesome Valley" (p. 69), and "The Gospel Train" (p141).

LESSON 42: BANJO STYLE PICKING: BASIC STRUM

Guitar and banjo finger picking techniques applied to the Autoharp will often overlap. Many of the banjo patterns are variations of broken arpeggio strums and Travis licks, but they are usually played faster and with only the thumb, index, and middle finger in the two higher octaves.*

Begin with the basic strum which can be practiced by using a downstroke in the middle octave with the index finger and an upward brush with the middle finger. It looks like this:

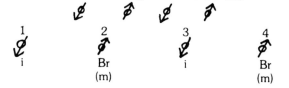

Fig. 56 Basic Banjo Strum

*For further study and more examples of these techniques, see Country Pickin' on the Autoharp by Meg Peterson, Mel Bay Publications.

This will seem awkward at first, since Autoharp players are not used to leading off with the index finger. Now add the thumb stroke which can be played in the lower octave, but is executed with more facility in the middle octave. The middle finger brush carries over onto a few strings of the higher octave. Otherwise, this is, basically, a middle octave strum.

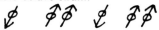

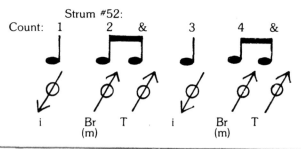

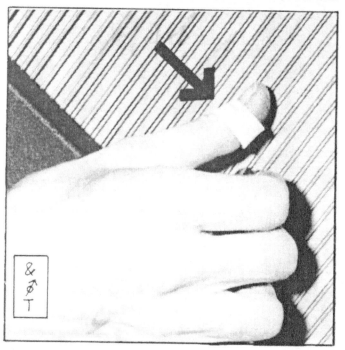

THE CRAWDAD SONG

Chords used: D, G, A7, G7, &D7

You get a line and I'll get a pole_____ hon-ey,

You get a line and I'll get a pole_____

(Continue Strum)

babe, You get a line and

I'll get a pole and we'll go down to the craw-dad hole

hon-ey_____ sug-ar ba - by mine._____

What you gonna do when the lake runs dry, honey?
What you gonna do when the lake runs dry, babe?
What you gonna do when the lake runs dry,
Sit on the banks and watch the crawdads die?
Honey, sugar baby mine.

USE OF HAMMERIN' ON

This next strum takes the basic pattern and substitutes hammerin' on (H) for the initial downstroke on the first beat. This is done very rapidly with the index finger. Strike the open strings on the count of "1," and press the chord down on the "&." Be sure your picks are on tight for this one.

Use hammerin' on every third or fourth measure only. It is a special effect to be used sparingly.

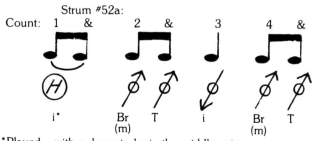

Strum #52a:

Count: 1 & 2 & 3 4 &

i*   Br T   i   Br T
     (m)   (m)

*Played with a downstroke in the middle octave.

139

BUFFALO GALS

Chords used: C, &G7

You can vary this basic strum, slow it down and use hammerin' on in the 2nd beat, in an adaptation of the Seegar style. The strum then becomes:

140

THE GOSPEL TRAIN
(Get On Board, Little Children)

Chords used: G, C, D7 & (Cm)

The gos-pel train is com-in', I hear it just at

hand,___ I hear the wheels a-mov-in' and

(Continue Strum)

(Chorus)

rumb-lin' thro' the land. Get on board, lit-tle

chil-dren; Get on board, lit-tle chil-dren; Get on

board, lit-tle chil-dren, there's room for man-y a more.

2. The fare is cheap and all can go,
The rich and poor are there;
No second class aboard this train,
No difference in the fare.   Chorus

3. I hear that train a-comin',
She sure is speedin' fast,
So get your tickets ready
And ride to heaven at last.   Chorus

FRAILING

Hammerin' on is also an important part of frailing, a right hand picking style traditional in the southern mountains. It varies from the basic strum in that the index finger strokes up on the first beat, heavily accented, instead of picking down. No picks are used, only the nails of the index and middle fingers. The (H) stroke is done rapidly on the 2nd half of the 1st beat, using either an up or a downstroke, depending on the facility of the player.

It is very difficult to transfer this technique to the Autoharp since it requires consecutive fast upstrokes with the index finger, middle finger, and thumb. Also, in frailing, the thumb plucks the highest banjo string whereas on the Autoharp it must play predominantly in the lower and middle octaves.

However, for those advanced players who wish to try, here's a challenging pattern which simulates frailing.

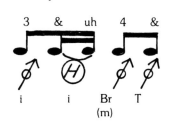

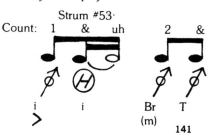

141

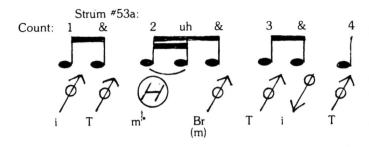

Strum #53a:

*Downstroke with the middle finger.

Now try the following strum which is a less complicated imitation of frailing, using strokes more suitable to the Autoharp, while retaining the feeling of the banjo sound.

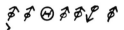

Play this last pattern on the following song.

JOHN HENRY

Chords used: C, F, G7, F7, D7, &Am

Good practice songs for these 4/4 strums are "Salty Dog," "Freight Train," "I've Got Peace Like A River" (p. 71), and "Cripple Creek."

LESSON 43: BANJO ROLLS INDEX FINGER LEAD

A guitar or banjo "roll" is a group of notes played consecutively in a pattern. They are usually the notes of a chord and are spaced evenly in an eighth note rhythm sequence. There are many possible rolls (such as backward and forward, two-finger, thumb and three finger, and thumb and alternating finger) several of which you have already played in previous sections of this book.

In the next strum the strings are picked in groups of three, giving the roll a syncopated beat. Accents are on the 1st, 4th, and 7th strokes. It may help to get the beat if you count:

1 - 2 - 3 - 4 - 5 - 6 - 7 - 8
>   >   >

rather than

1 - & - 2 - & - 3 - & - 4 - &
>   >   >

Notice the finger pattern, which leads off with the index finger.

i m T i m T i m

Strum #54:

Count: 1 & 2 & 3 & 4 &

i m T i m T i m

As you practice, increase the tempo and you'll find that you
have to play closer together in the middle or the higher octave.

EVERY TIME I FEEL THE SPIRIT

Chords used: C, F, &G7

Chorus: Ev' - ry   time   I   feel   the   spi - rit   Mov - in'

(Continue Strum)

in my heart_____   I   will   pray,_____   Ev' - ry

time   I   feel   the   spi - rit   mov - in' in my heart   I   will

pray.   Verse: U-pon the   moun - tain,   when my Lord spoke,   Out of his

mouth came___ fire   and   smoke;   Look'd all a - round me   it looked so

fine_____   'Til   I   asked   my   Lord   if   all   were mine.

In the next strum the index finger leads off again, but this time
with an upstroke brush. This fast strum is executed better without
picks. The index fingernail is used for the brush and the thumb
alternates between the middle and the lower octaves.

The finger pattern now becomes: i m i T i m i T

Strum #54a:

Count: 1 &   2 &   3 &   4 &

Br m   i   T   Br m   i   T
(i)   (i)

143

This next song is made especially interesting by rapid chord changes in the middle of the pattern. Notice how the changes also produce a melody line. Use two complete strum patterns per measure.

GRANDFATHER'S CLOCK

Chords used: G, C, D7, & Am

My grand - fath - er's clock was too large for the shelf, So it stood nine-ty years on the floor_____ It was tall - er by half than the old man him-self, 'though it weighed not a pen - ny weight more It was bought on the morn of the day that he was born, And was al - ways his pride and his joy But it stopped short nev-er to go a-gain, when the old man died. Nine-ty years with-out slum-ber-ing tick, tock, tick, tock; His life sec-onds num-ber-ing tick, tock, tick, tock; It stopped short nev-er to go a-gain, when the old man died

THUMB LEAD

In this next pattern the thumb leads off in the lower part of the middle octave, moves to the lower octave, and comes back to the middle octave. It alternates with two downstrokes played by the index and middle finger. The strum is made interesting by the reversal of the order of the two finger strokes as they go from lower to higher and back again. This can be played as a straight country strum, or with an accent on the 1st, 4th, and 7th strokes as in Strum #54.

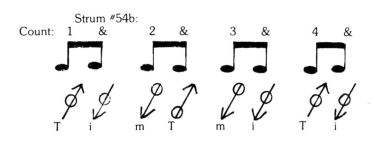

CAMPTOWN RACES

Practice songs for this rolls include "Cumberland Gap",
"These Bones Gonna Rise Again", and "Wildwood Flower" (p.74).

Stephen Foster

Chords used: D, G, A7, & D7

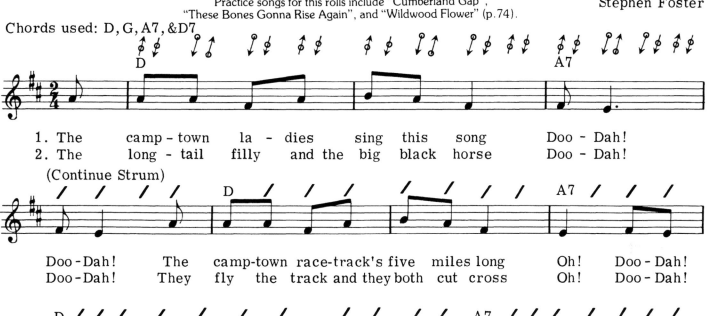

1. The camp-town la-dies sing this song Doo-Dah!
2. The long-tail filly and the big black horse Doo-Dah!

(Continue Strum)

Doo-Dah! The camp-town race-track's five miles long Oh! Doo-Dah!
Doo-Dah! They fly the track and they both cut cross Oh! Doo-Dah!

day; I came down there with my hat caved in Doo-Dah! Doo-Dah! I
day; The blind horse stuck in a big mud hole Doo-Dah! Doo-Dah! He

go back home with a pocketful of tin Oh! Doo-Dah! day!
can't touch bottom with a ten-foot pole Oh! Doo-Dah! day!

Chorus

Goin' to run all night! Goin' to run all day! I'll

bet my mon-ey on the bob-tail nag Some-bod-y bet on the bay.

The longtail filly and the big black horse   Doo-Dah! Doo-Dah!
They fly the track and they both cut a cross   Oh! Doo-Dah day.
The blind horse stuck in a big mud hole   Doo-Dah! Doo-Dah!
He can't touch bottom with a ten foot pole   Oh! Doo-Dah day.
Chorus

LESSON 44: BANJO ROLLS USING THE PINCH

The Pinch is incorporated as part of a triplet figure in this next roll. The index finger leads off in the triplet and completes the pattern with an arpeggiando in the middle and higher octave. The thumb alternates, playing the lowest strings on the count of "one" and moving higher on the count of "three."

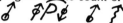

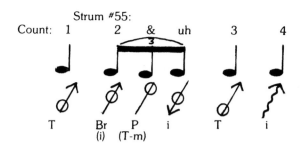

OLD TIME RELIGION
(21 chord model)

Chords used: G, C, D7, Em & B7

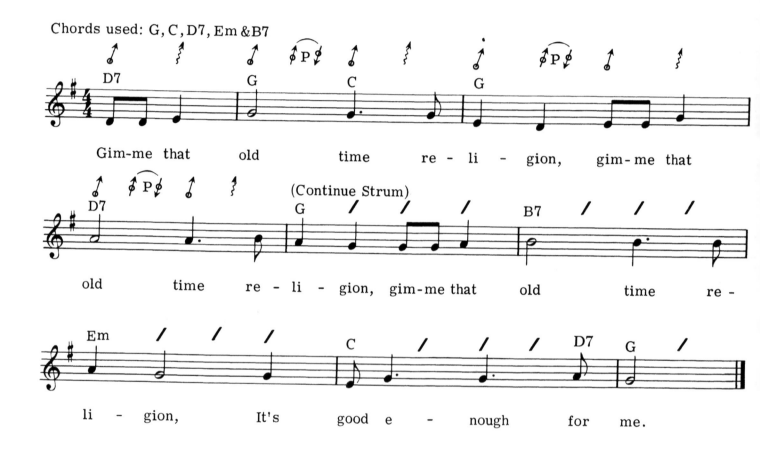

Gim-me that old time re - li - gion, gim-me that

old time re - li - gion, gim-me that old time re -

li - gion, It's good e - nough for me.

2. It was good for the Hebrew children,
   It was good for the Hebrew children,
   It was good for the Hebrew children,
   It's good enough for me.

In this next pattern the thumb leads off in the triplet, and the Pinch is similar to the double stops in lessons 39 and 40 (p127). However, it is fuller, using the thumb, index, and middle finger) (T-i-m), rather than the index, middle, and ring finger (i-m-r). The thumb continues its alternating pattern.

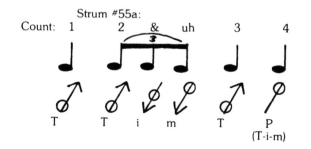

Picks are used effectively with this old tune.

OLD DAN TUCKER

Chords used: G,C,&D7

Went to town the oth – er night to hear a noise and

see a fight. All the peo-ple were a run-ning a-round, Cry-ing

"Old Dan Tuck-er's come to town." Chorus: Get out the way,

Old Dan Tuck-er, You're too late to come for sup-per,

Sup - per's o - ver and din - ner's cook - in, And

Old Dan Tuck - er just stand - in' there look - in'.

SYNCOPATED PATTERNS

The Pinch leads off in the next pattern, and the beat is similar to the rocker strum used on old blues melodies, except that the tempo is faster and the rhythm syncopated.

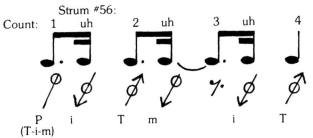

Strum #56:

Count: 1 uh 2 uh 3 uh 4

P i T m i T
(T-i-m)

It takes real concentration to play this accompaniment against this melody.

GOIN' DOWN THE ROAD FEELIN' BAD

Chords used: D, G, A7, D7, & G7

I'm go-in' down the road feel-ing bad, Oh Lord, I'm

(Continue Strum)

go-in' down the road feel-ing bad._____ I'm

go-in' down the road feel-ing bad, Lord, Lord,__ And I

ain't gon - na be treat-ed this a - way._____

2. I'm goin' where the climate suits my clothes (3 times)
And I'm sure gonna be feelin' better soon.

A slightly different feeling is created when eighth and quarter notes are used, and there is no accent.

*Hammerin' On Ⓗ can be used very effectively in place of this downstroke. The "ah-um" will carry over into the 3rd beat "rest."

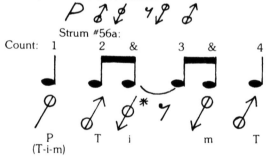

Strum #56a:

Count: 1   2   &   3   &   4

P   T   i   m   T
(T-i-m)

LET MY LITTLE LIGHT SHINE
(21 and 27 chord model)

Chords used: G, C, D7, A7, G7, C7, B7, & Em

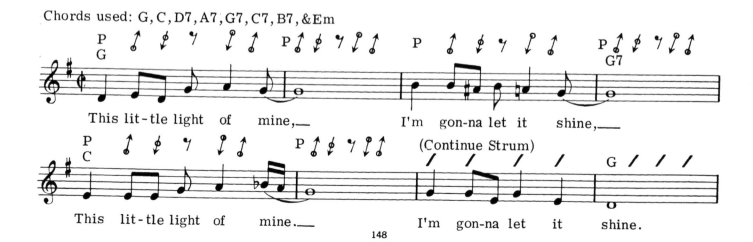

This lit-tle light of mine,__ I'm gon-na let it shine,__

(Continue Strum)

This lit-tle light of mine.__ I'm gon-na let it shine.

148

This lit-tle light of mine,___ I'm gon-na let it shine,___ ev-'ry
day, ev-'ry day, ev-'ry day, ev - 'ry day,___ gon-na
let my lit-tle light shine._____ On Mon-day he gave me the gift_
___ of love. On Tues-day peace came from a-bove. On Wednes-day told me to
have more faith. On Thurs-day gave me a lit-tle more grace. On
Fri-day told me to watch and pray. On Sat-ur-day told me just what to say. On
Sun-day gave me the pow-er di - vine, just to let my lit-tle light shine.

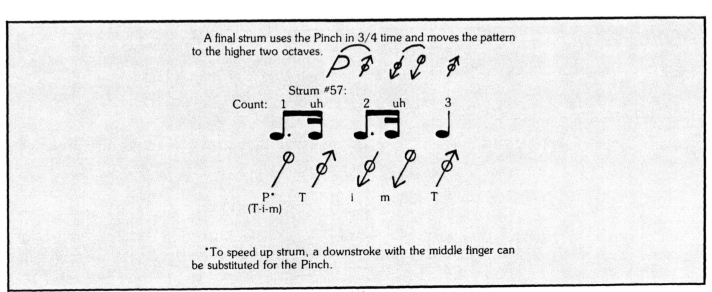

A final strum uses the Pinch in 3/4 time and moves the pattern
to the higher two octaves.

Strum #57:
Count: 1 uh 2 uh 3

P T i m T
(T-i-m)

*To speed up strum, a downstroke with the middle finger can
be substituted for the Pinch.

BEAUTIFUL BROWN EYES

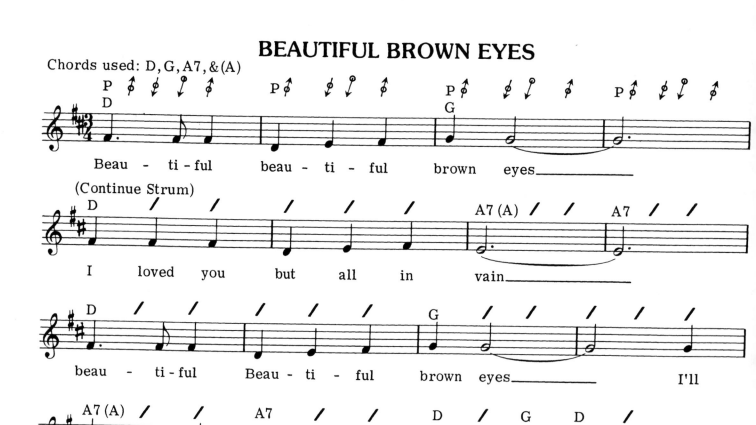

Chords used: D, G, A7, & (A)

Beau - ti - ful beau - ti - ful brown eyes_____

(Continue Strum)

I loved you but all in vain_____

beau - ti - ful Beau - ti - ful brown eyes_____ I'll

ne - ver love blue eyes a - gain_____

Good 3/4 practice songs include "Rye Whiskey" and "Green Grow The Lilacs". Other 4/4 songs are "Rosewood Casket", "The Roving Gambler", "Bury Me Beneath The Willow", "Black Eyed Susie", and "Shoo Fly" (p.155).

LESSON 45: ADVANCED STRUMS FIVE FINGER PICKING

This next pattern uses descending and ascending pinches and all five fingers. It is fast and requires a great deal of practice to strengthen the ring and little finger pinches.

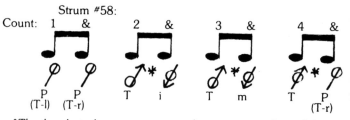

*The thumb stroke moves up on each successive stroke and the index and middle finger alternate on different sections of the middle octave.

I KNOW WHERE I'M GOIN'

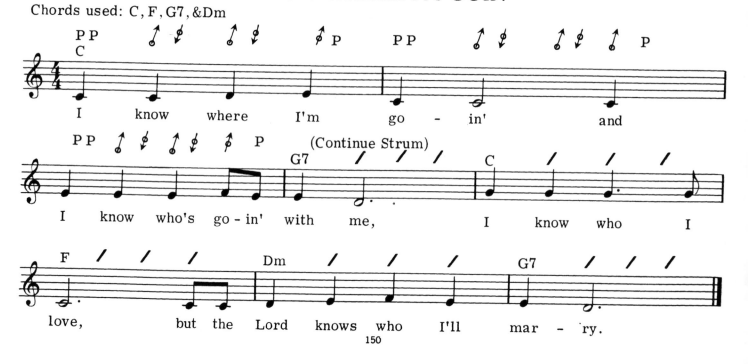

Chords used: C, F, G7, & Dm

I know where I'm go - in' and

I know who's go - in' with me, I know who I

love, but the Lord knows who I'll mar - ry.

Now that you are familiar with the pattern, speed it up and play two complete strums in each measure on the following tune. Continue to count in 8th notes, rather than changing to 16th notes, which would make counting and notation awkward.

Notice as you play that you change chords frequently in the middle of a strum pattern. Also, you will be playing even 8th notes over the uneven melody on such words as "bon-nie."

LOCH LOMOND

words by Lady John Scott
Scottish melody

An interesting variation of this pattern would be to substitute a Rasgueado Backwards (RB, p. 85) for the Pinch on the 2nd half of the 1st beat.

The next song is chorded for melody but the numbers of the strings are omitted. It is not necessary to hit the exact melody string while using the strum pattern. You can enrich the sound by including the middle finger in the pinches, almost like a double stop. As you do two complete strum patterns per measure, notice how you can play the melody an octave higher, using the pinches, or pick it out on the lower strings with the thumb and alternating index and middle finger. You can alter the pattern, occasionally, to make it fit the melody more closely. By now your ear will help you figure out the tune.

BATTLE HYMN OF THE REPUBLIC

Chords used: C, F, G7, E7, C7, Am, & Dm

Mine eyes have seen the glo - ry of the

com - ing of the Lord; He is tramp - ling out the vin - tage where the

grapes of wrath are stored; He has loos'd the fate - ful light - ning of His

ter - ri-ble swift sword, His truth is march - ing on.

Glo - ry, glo - ry hal - le - lu - jah!

Glo - ry, glo - ry hal - le - lu - jah! Glo - ry, glo - ry hal - le -

lu - jah! His truth is march - ing on._____

152

When you have learned this arrangement, play it again using the tapping stroke (p.112) on each beat. Even without picking the actual melody it will be easily recognizable by using the frequent chord changes. If the Autoharp is amplified it will be even more effective.

Other songs that lend themselves to five finger picking are "Lonesome Road" (p. 21), "Will the Circle Be Unbroken", "Mama Don't 'Low," and "Lonesome Valley" (p.69).

A 3/4 variation of this pattern uses pinches with the thumb and middle (T-m) and thumb and index (T-i) fingers.

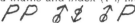

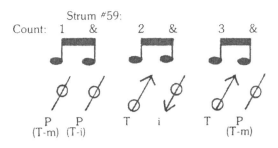

> Using smaller pinches fits into the next melody because the tune is in the lower two octaves. If you wish to play it an octave higher, return to the original pattern of pinches, (T-l) and (T-r) in the higher octave. Use only one strum pattern in each measure.

THE BAND PLAYED ON

Chords used: G, C, D7, G7, E7, Am, (Em) & (C#dim.)

Good practice songs in 3/4 time are "My Bonnie" (p.39), "The Rose of Tralee", "My Wild Irish Rose", "Home On The Range" (p.41), and "Sweet Betsy From Pike" (p.43).

153

LESSON 46: ADVANCED STRUMS: MELODY WITH BROKEN ARPEGGIO STRUMS

There are many varieties of 5 finger picking that can be used to play melody on the Autoharp. Here is one pattern which uses a flowing broken arpeggio with the thumb hitting the melody string most of the time. The frequent chord changes help bring out the melody even when the exact string is not plucked.

Since the melody starts in the middle octave the entire strum will be played in the top two octaves.

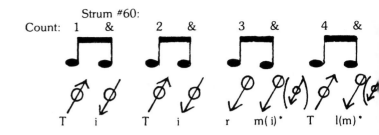

*These are alternate fingerings which may simplify the pattern for some players.

THE CRUEL WAR
(21 and 27 chord model)

Chords used: G, C, D7, Am, Em & B7

1. The cruel war is rag-ing, John-ny has to fight; I____
want to be with him from morn-ing 'til night. I
want to be with Him, It grives__ my heart so; "Won't you
let me go with you?" "No, my love no."

2. Tomorrow is Sunday, Monday is the day;
   That your captain will call you, And you must obey.
   Your captain will call you, It grieves my heart so:
   "Won't you let me go with you? No, My love no."

3. I'll tie back my hair; Men's clothing I'll put on;
   I'll pass as your comrade, As we march along.
   I'll pass as your comrade, No one will ever know;
   "Won't you let me go with you? No, My love no."

Here is another strum which moves to the lower octave. Play the same song an octave lower, starting on the 4th string. Remember to be flexible in following the octave designations. They're only guidelines and may change, slightly, to accommodate the melody. The thumb will move up in the lower octave whenever necessary to keep the melody going.

Ignore the string numbers and play the song by ear.

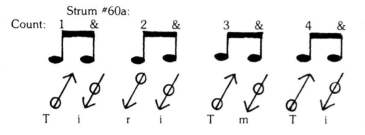

Strum #60a:
Count: 1 & 2 & 3 & 4 &

T i r i T m T i

MELODY WITH SYNCOPATED STRUM

This next song could be played with the two previous patterns, but syncopation gives it more zip. By now you are proficient enough to juggle the pattern slightly when it may not conform to the melody, or even alter the original rhythm to add interest and variety whenever the pause coincides with a chord change.

There are no octave designations because the placement of the fingers depends on the individual melody notes. You may play them as written or an octave lower. The thumb does most of the melody picking while the other fingers fill in with the rhythm.

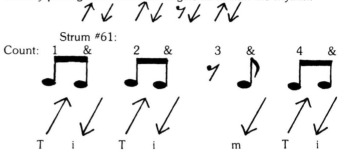

Strum #61:
Count: 1 & 2 & 3 & 4 &

T i T i m T i

You'll notice that a new key is used in this next song; the key of Eb major. Its principal chords are Eb, Ab, and Bb7.

SHOO FLY
(21 and 27 chord model)

Key of Eb
Eb, Ab, & Bb7

Chords used: Eb, Ab, Bb7, & Bb

For those who wish to try another excellent pattern on this song, see Strum #25, p103 It will not be as accurate in reproducing the melody, but fitting the pattern with the fast changes is challenging, making the total effect exciting.

LESSON 47: ADVANCED STRUMS: COMBINED WITH THE PINCH

In this next strum a wide pinch is combined with two finger strokes in a triplet figure. With each pinch the middle finger picks the high melody string and the index finger and thumb keep the rhythm going.

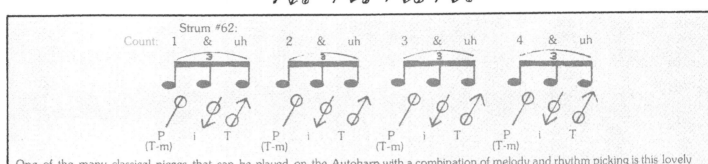

One of the many classical pieces that can be played on the Autoharp with a combination of melody and rhythm picking is this lovely excerpt from "Beethoven's 9th Symphony."

ODE TO JOY

Beethoven

Chords used: C, F, G7, G, Am, & D7

This strum calls for wide pinches with the thumb and middle finger, encompassing all three octaves. It is played rapidly, using two complete patterns in every measure.

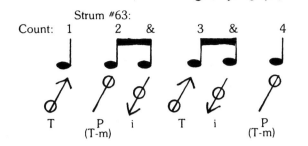

Strum #63:

Once you have perfected this strum you can experiment with smaller pinches and a variety of alternating finger strokes. The range of possible combinations is almost limitless.

The following old folk song introduces the principal chords in the key of A major: A, D, & E7.

Key of A
A, D, & E7

Those of you who do not own a 21 or 27 chord instrument can play in the key of C, using C, F, G7, and D7 (See Transposition Chart, p.164).

THE WRECK OF THE OLD NINETY-SEVEN
(21 and 27 chord model)

Chords used: A, D, E7, A7, & B7

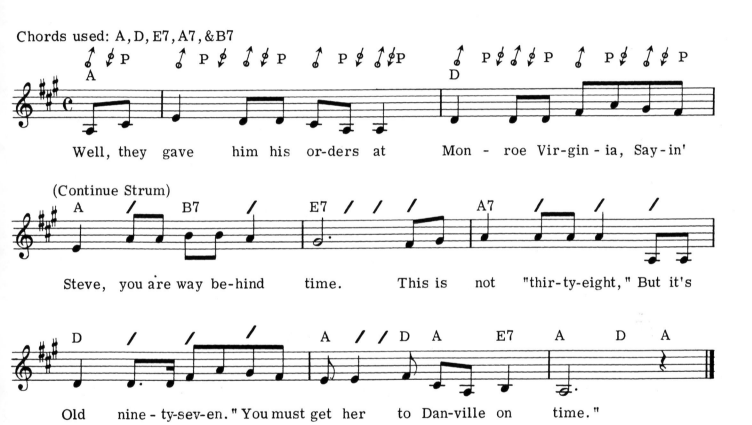

Well, they gave him his or-ders at Mon - roe Vir-gin - ia, Say-in'

Steve, you are way be-hind time. This is not "thir-ty-eight," But it's

Old nine - ty-sev-en." You must get her to Dan-ville on time."

He turned and said to his black greasy fireman,
"Just shovel on a little more coal,
And when we cross the White Oak Mountain
You can watch old 'ninety-seven' roll."

It's a mighty rough road from Lynchburg to Danville,
On a line on a three mile grade,
It was on this grade that he lost his average,
You can see what a jump he made.

He was going down the grade makin' ninety miles an hour,
When his whistle broke into a scream,
They found him in the wreck
With his hand on the throttle, he was scalded to death by steam.

Now, ladies, you must take warning,
From this time now on learn,
Never speak harsh words to your true loving husband,
He may leave you and never return.

157

LESSON 48: POPULAR CHORD SEQUENCES

Here are four basic sequences used to play popular music from the Gay Nineties through the '50's and into the '70's. The strum you choose depends on the era in which the song was popular and the feeling you wish to convey. Just by changing the rhythm and the tempo you can bring to mind a whole new song.

The first sequence was very popular in the '20's, and has remained so with such hits as "Ja-da", "Walk Right In", and John Sebastian's "What A Day For A Daydream". The number of strum patterns per measure, or the length of time you stay on each chord, depends on the song. Let your ear be your judge!

Each sequence will be written in the keys of C and F.

> C - A7 - D7 - G7 C
> OR:
> F - D7 - G7 - C7 - F

Try both keys using a syncopated version of the shuffle rhythm.

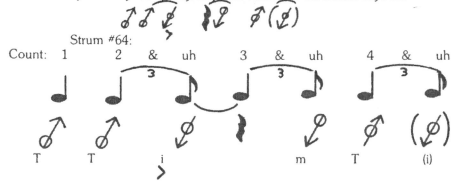

To add interest change the last 2 beats to small descending pinches and transfer the accent to the first pinch.

The first pinch is wide and the others are small. It's more effective if you alternate these two patterns so the pinches won't become monotonous.

The second sequence is probably most familiar. It calls to mind such songs as "Five Foot Two," "Hey, Look Me Over," "Anytime," "Shanty Town," "Alice's Restaurant," and "The Last Time I Saw Him." Many contemporary composers of pop music use this sequence in their tunes. See if you can think of some to go along with the next three strum patterns.

> C - E7 - A7 - D7 - G7 - C
>
> OR:
>
> F - A7 - D7 - G7 - C7 - F

Try another syncopated version of the triplet rhythm.

The next variation adds the pinch and three strokes on the last full beat.

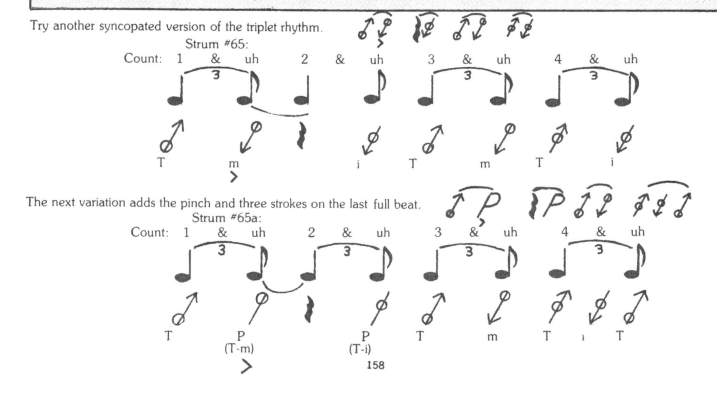

158

One last pattern for this sequence is very dramatic when played fast. It leaves out the stroke on the 2nd beat and accents the 3rd.

This is a very popular rock beat.

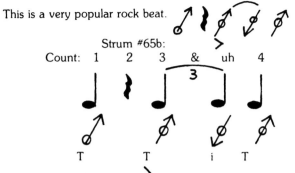

Strum #65b:
Count: 1   2   3   &   uh   4

The third sequence provides the basic harmony for such songs as "Red Roses For A Blue Lady." Notice that I've added a new 7th chord in each successive sequence.

| C - B7 - E7 - A7 - D7 - G7 - C |
| OR: |
| F - E7 - A7 - D7 - G7 - C7 - F |

This strum uses small descending pinches with a Travis pattern in rocker rhythm on the last four strokes. The pinches alternate, as in Strum #64, between thumb and middle (T-m) and thumb and index finger (T-i). The pinches are all small, however, and should be played in slightly different sections of the octaves, going from the higher to the lower strings.

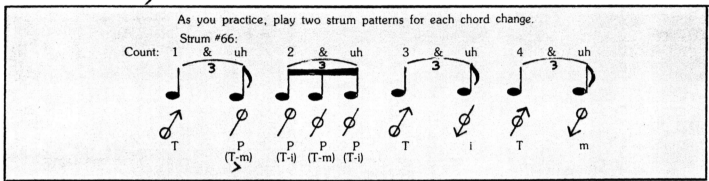

As you practice, play two strum patterns for each chord change.

Strum #66:
Count: 1   &   uh   2   &   uh   3   &   uh   4   &   uh

Other patterns that adapt themselves well to those three chord sequences are Strum #23c (p.101) and Strum #26 (p.104).

The final sequence uses a 4 measure strum pattern similar to those popularized by the Credence Clearwater rock group. It is a typical rock sequence sounding best when amplified and played with a heavy beat. It can be moved, completely, to the lower octave and played just as effectively as a triplet rhythm.

The brush stroke (Br) is heavier than in mountain strumming (p.32). The thumb lifts off and returns to the lowest strings before starting the stroke. It is actually a combination brush and arpeggiando stroke. Notice that only the thumb and index finger are used, both of which should have picks.

The chord changes for C and F are written above the pattern. F is on the top line and C is on the bottom.

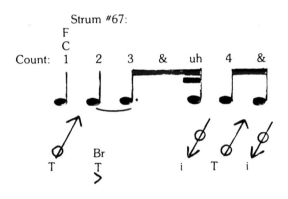

Strum #67:
F
C
Count: 1   2   3   &   uh   4   &

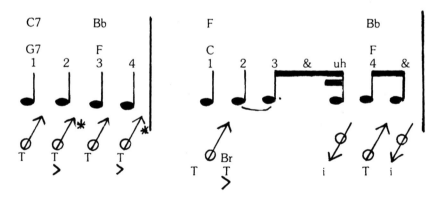

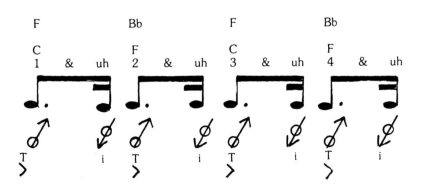

*Alternating thumb stroke played in slightly higher section of the lower octave.

159

MAJOR SCALE

A MAJOR SCALE IS A SERIES OF EIGHT NOTES ARRANGED IN A PATTERN OF WHOLE STEPS AND HALF STEPS. TO CONSTRUCT A MAJOR SCALE WE FIRST START WITH THE NAME OF THE SCALE (Frequently called the Root or Tonic). WITH THE C SCALE THIS WOULD BE THE NOTE "C". THE REST OF THE SCALE WOULD FALL IN LINE AS FOLLOWS:

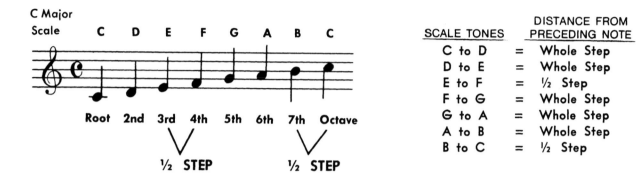

SCALE TONES		DISTANCE FROM PRECEDING NOTE
C to D	=	Whole Step
D to E	=	Whole Step
E to F	=	½ Step
F to G	=	Whole Step
G to A	=	Whole Step
A to B	=	Whole Step
B to C	=	½ Step

G MAJOR SCALE

SCALE TONES		DISTANCE FROM PRECEDING NOTE
ROOT	(C)	
2nd	(D)	WHOLE STEP
3rd	(E)	WHOLE STEP
4th	(F)	½ STEP
5th	(G)	WHOLE STEP
6th	(A)	WHOLE STEP
7th	(B)	WHOLE STEP
Octave	(C)	½ STEP

WITH THE ABOVE FORMULA YOU CAN CONSTRUCT ANY MAJOR SCALE!

TO CONSTRUCT THE G MAJOR SCALE, START WITH THE NOTE G, CONSTRUCT IT AS FOLLOWS:

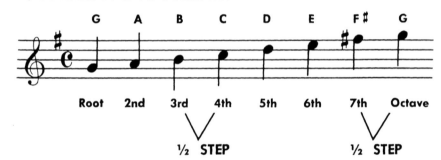

NOTICE THAT IN ORDER TO MAKE OUR FORMULA WORK WITH THE G SCALE WE MUST SHARP (#) THE F. THERE MUST BE A WHOLE STEP BETWEEN THE 6th AND 7th TONES OF THE SCALE. IN ORDER TO ESTABLISH A WHOLE STEP BETWEEN E AND F WE MUST SHARP THE F.

MINOR SCALE

Many types of Minor Scales exist. For our purposes of chord construction, we will be dealing with the pure Minor Scale. The Formula for building a pure Minor Scale is as follows:

Find the 6th Tone of a Major Scale and continue through eight letters of that Major Scale. If we take the C Scale for example, we will find that A is the 6th Tone of the C Scale. If we then start with A and continue for eight notes, we will have the A Minor Scale.

"A" Minor is said to be "Relative" to C. (A is the 6th Tone in the C Scale and the A Minor Scale is built on the scale starting with A.)

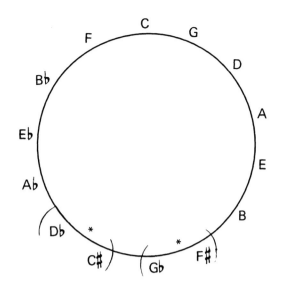

HOW TO FIND THE CHORDS

The three principal chords are:

        TONIC   SUB DOMINANT and DOMINANT 7TH
    or   1(I)   4(IV)   and   5(V₇)

Pick out any chord on the circle. This is the tonic chord. Now move counterclockwise to the next chord. This is the sub dominant chord.

The first chord clockwise to the tonic is the dominant 7th chord.

The dominant 7th naturally is a seventh chord.

As an example the chords in the key of C are C, F and G7.

In the key of G: G, C and D7 or the key of E: E, A and B7.

You now know enough chords to play in the keys of C, G, D, A and E.

MAJOR CHORDS

A Major Chord is comprised of the Root, 3rd, and 5th tones of a scale. The notes in the C major chord would be C - E - G. The notes in the G chord are G - B - D.

Write the Notes of the Major Chords and Label as Folows:

Example:

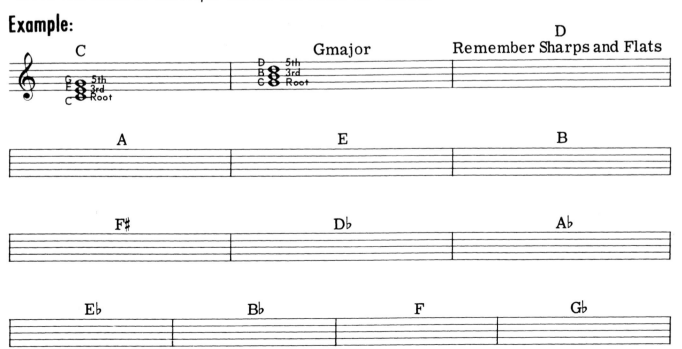

MINOR CHORDS

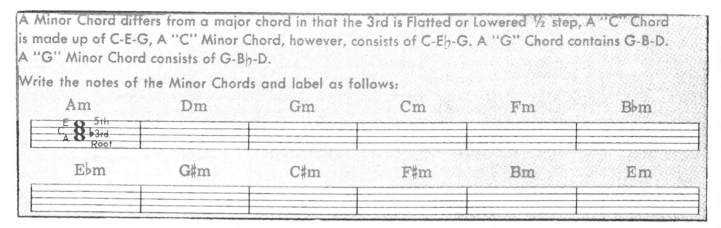

A Minor Chord differs from a major chord in that the 3rd is Flatted or Lowered ½ step. A "C" Chord is made up of C-E-G. A "C" Minor Chord, however, consists of C-E♭-G. A "G" Chord contains G-B-D. A "G" Minor Chord consists of G-B♭-D.

Write the notes of the Minor Chords and label as follows:

DOMINANT SEVENTH CHORDS

A Dominant Seventh Chord is comprised of the Root, 3rd, 5th and Flatted or lowered Seventh. The notes in the C dominant Seventh chord, for example, are C - E - G - B♭. You will note that B♮ is the seventh tone in the C scale; however, our rule for constructing the seventh chord tells us to Flat or lower the seventh tone. Thus B♭ is the desired note. We will call Dominant Seventh Chords Seventh Chords. (E7, C7, B7, etc.)

Construct the Seventh Chord as follows:

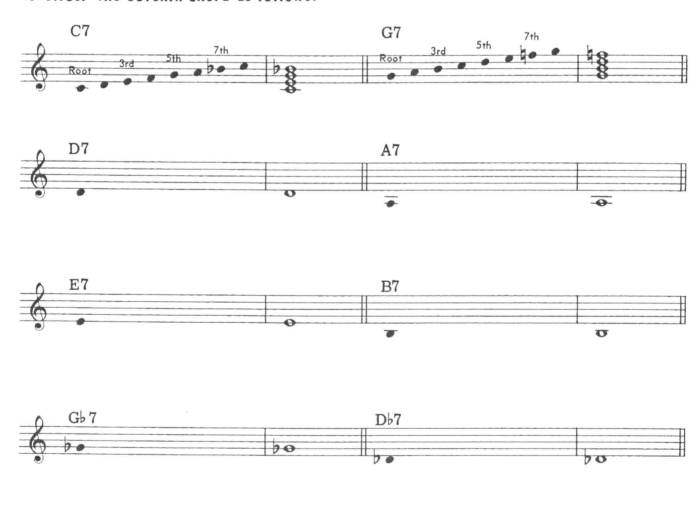

CHORD ARRANGEMENTS

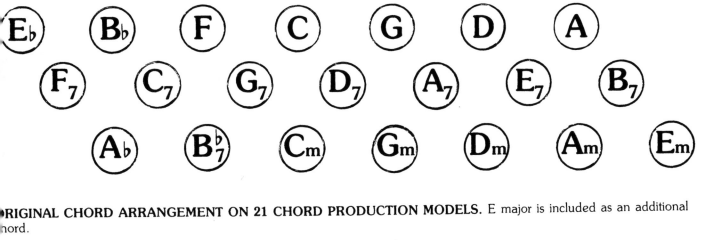

ORIGINAL CHORD ARRANGEMENT ON 21 CHORD PRODUCTION MODELS. E major is included as an additional chord.

Majors on the top row, minors on the bottom row and 7ths in the middle row.

or E

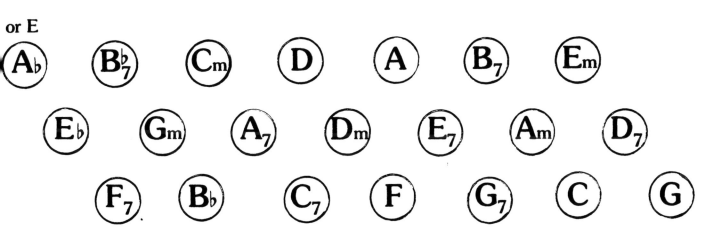

ALTERNATE CHORD ARRANGEMENT #1 FOR 21 CHORD AUTOHARP. E major would be included as an additional chord and could be substituted for the Ab major, as shown above, or any other chord not frequently used.

This is the arrangement I use, for it is similar to the 15 chord instrument. Those who use both models can see how easy it is to go from one model to the other without having to learn different chord locations.

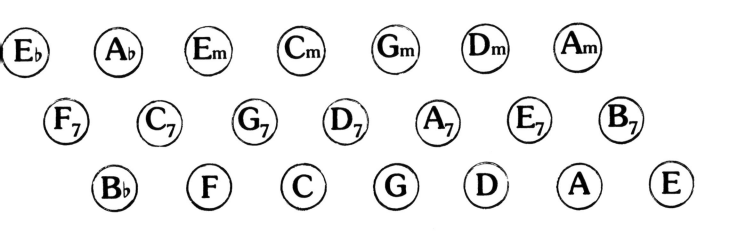

ALTERNATE CHORD ARRANGEMENT #2 FOR 21 CHORD AUTOHARP. Major chords on bottom line, minor chords on the top line, 7th chords in the middle line.

Bb7 would be included as an additional chord, and could be substituted for any chord not frequently used.

163

To change the chord arrangement on a 21 chord instrument unscrew the plastic lid covering the chords and move the bars to whatever location is desired (See Fig. B).

Fig. B

Fig. C

Each chord bar is grooved and has a plastic button which slides back and forth in the groove. It can be moved to any location on the chord bar to fit into any of the three rows of holes in the chord bar cover (See Fig. C).

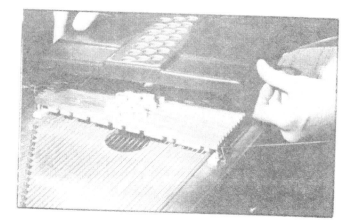

Fig. D

Fig. E

Fig. F

After rearranging the chord bars, put the plastic chord bar cover back in place. Buttons must be carefully lined up before the cover can be properly screwed down (See Fig. D, E, and F).

To understand the relationship of one chord to another, both the 15 and 21 chord models have convenient chord arrangements. The three principal chords in each key are grouped so that the interrelationship of one key to another can be seen immediately, thus facilitating the study of harmony and the playing of the instrument (See Figures G and H).

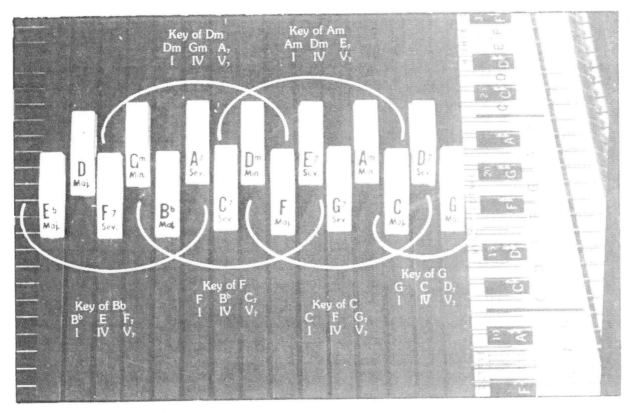

Fig. G (15 chord model)

Fig. H (21 chord model)

163B

TRANSPOSITION

Transposition is the process of putting a song into a key other than the original, for simplifying the playing and/or singing of the song:

The following chart can be used for transposing the chords and/or the melody of a song:

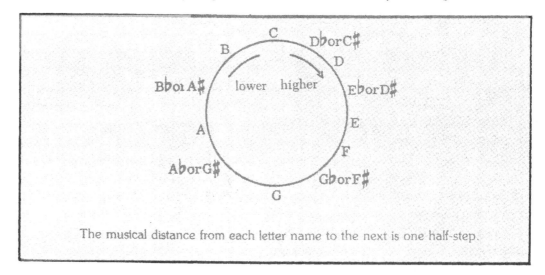

The musical distance from each letter name to the next is one half-step.

As an example of transposition, start with the following melody:

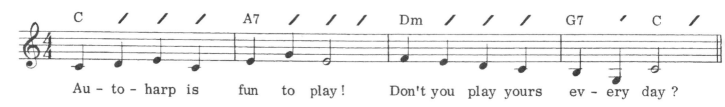

Many people would find this melody too low to sing comfortably. Using the chart, the song can be transposed to a higher key.

The song is written in the key of C. For this example, it will be transposed to the key of F. Starting on C, move clockwise around the wheel to F. Not counting C, the starting point, there are 5 letter names (or half-steps) from C to F. Thus, the same procedure can be used with all of the chords and notes in the song, to result in a version of the song in the key of F:

Notice that the chord types do not change, just their letter names: In other words, 7th chords remain 7th chords, minor chords remain minor, and major chords remain major.

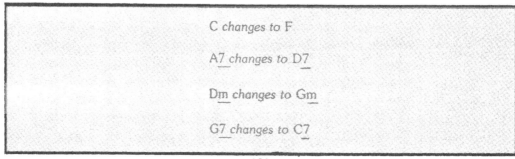

Transposition may also be used when a song, due to its key, is not playable on the Autoharp:

| Gb / / / | Eb7 / / / | Abm / / / | Db7 / Gb / |

Au - to - harp is   fun   to   play!   Don't you   play yours   ev - ery   day ?

This version of the song is in the key of G♭, which cannot be played on the Autoharp. However, if all the chords and notes are raised one half-step (one letter name clockwise) the song will be transposed to the key of G, which is playable on all Autoharps:

| G / / / | E7 / / / | Am / / / | D7 / G / |

Au - to - harp   is   fun   to   play!   Don't you   play yours   ev - ery   day ?

Sample transposition exercises:

1) Transpose the following chord progression two half-steps higher:
   F   F7   B♭   Gm   C7   F

2) Transpose the following chord progression to nearest playable key:
   D♭   D♭7   G♭   A♭7   D♭

3) Transpose the following chord progression one half-step higher:
   E   A   E   A   B7   E

Answers to above exercises:

1) G   G7   C   Am   D7   G
2) C   C7   F   G7   C
               or
   D   D7   G   A7   D
3) F   B♭   F   B♭   C7   F

CHORD SUBSTITUTIONS

Sometimes a chord is called for that does not exist on the Autoharp. If the chord is major, minor, or 7th, here's what to do.

Written chord	Possible substitutes
Ab	Cm
Db or C#	no acceptable chord
Gb or F#	no acceptable chord
B	no acceptable chord
E	E7
A	A7
Cm	Eb
Fm	Ab
Bbm	no acceptable chord
Ebm	no acceptable chord
Abm or G#m	E
Dbm or C#m	E or A
Gbm	A or D
Bm	D or G
Em	G or C
Bb7	E7
Eb7	A7
Ab7 or G#7	D7
Db7 or C#7	G7
Gb7 or F#7	C7
B7	F7

With the exception of augmented (+) and diminished (°) chords, all others can be simplified to the three categories above:
6th, major 7th, 6/9, major 9th are major.
m6, m7, m+7, m6/9, m9, m11, are minor.
7-5, 7+5, 9, 7-9, 7+9, 11, 13 are 7ths.

Both augmented and diminished chords can be replaced by 7ths, but *each substitute chord must be tested by ear*, as its effect varies depending on the context.

Written chord	Possible substitutes
C, D#, Eb, F#, Gb, or A diminished	F7, B7, D7
C#, Db, E, G, A#, or Bb diminished	A7, C7
D, F, G#, Ab, or B diminished	G7, Bb7, E7
C, E, G#, or Ab augmented	C7, E7, D7
C#, Db, F, or A augmented	F7, A7, G7
D, F#, A#, or Bb augmented	D7, Bb7, C7
Eb, G, or B augmented	G7, F7, A7

General note

Substitute chords rarely, if ever, sound as good as the correct chord. It is usually better to transpose the arrangement to a different key. For example, if a song in the key of F has the chords F and Db, you will find it impossible to play. If, however, the song is transposed to the key of G, the same two chords become G and Eb. (See transposition chart, p.164).

Melody Aids*

*Used by permission of Music Education Group, Union N.J. From "Teaching Music With The Autoharp,"Robert E. Nye, Meg Peterson.

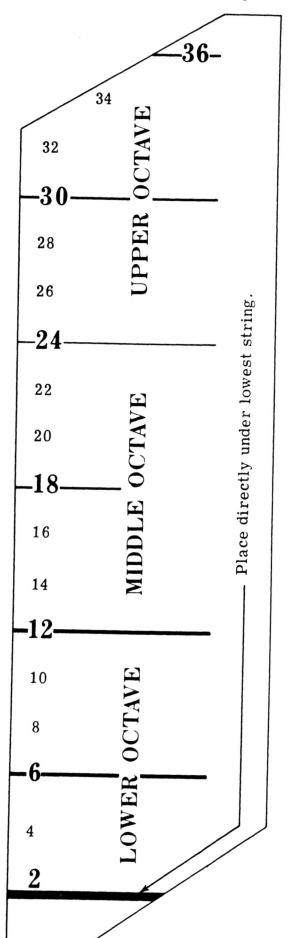

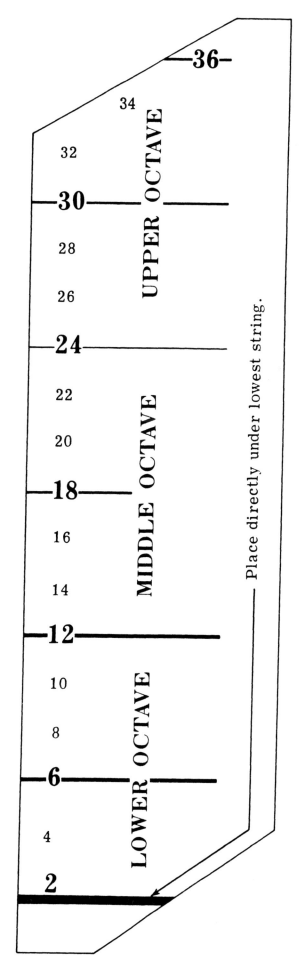

ALPHABETICAL INDEX OF SONGS

LIST OF PUBLICATIONS BY MEG PETERSON

AUTOHARP PRAISE ; Mel Bay Publications

THE COMPLETE METHOD FOR AUTOHARP OR CHROMAHARP; Mel Bay Publications 1979
    TEACHING CASSETTE

LET'S PLAY THE AUTOHARP & CHROMAHARP! New ways to introduce and play the basic strums; Mel Bay 1980

SONGS FOR THE AUTOHARP (ALL TIME FAVORITES), Meg Peterson & Dan Fox; Mel Bay Publications

MORE SONGS FOR AUTOHARP , Meg Peterson & Dan Fox; Mel Bay Publications 1980

HYMNS FOR THE AUTOHARP; Mel Bay Publications 1978

SONGS OF CHRISTMAS FOR AUTOHARP, Meg Peterson & Dan Fox; Mel Bay Publications 1980

COUNTRY PICKING ON THE AUTOHARP*Mel Bay Publications, (1984)

THE BEATLES' GREATEST HITS; Cherry Lane Music Co. 1979

THE MANY WAYS TO PLAY THE AUTOHARP, Oscar Schmidt International, Inc. 1966
    Vol. 1—Beginning Techniques
    Vol. 2—Advanced Techniques

AUTOHARP PARADE: Oscar Schmidt International, Inc. 1967
    VOL. 1—100 FAVORITE SONGS FOR YOUNG PEOPLE
    VOL. 2—100 WORLD'S BEST LOVED SONGS
    VOL. 3—100 HYMNS AND SPIRITUALS

SESAME STREET SONGBOOK; Warner Brothers Publications, Inc. 1970

TEACHING MUSIC WITH THE AUTOHARP :New revised edition, 1982.

AUTOHARP ANTHOLOGY; MCA/Mills 1976
    "POP" CLASSICS: 27 HITS OF OUR TIME
    NOSTALGIA: 27 OLDIES BUT GOODIES

JOHN DENVER'S GREATEST HITS; Cherry Lane Music Co. 1977
    MOUNTAIN AND ARPEGGIO STRUMS
    MELODY AND TRAVIS PICKING

ELEMENTARY MUSIC FOR ALL LEARNERS, written in collaboration with Dr. Rosalie Pratt. Alfred Publications 1980
    (available with student workbook, sets of charts and 3 LP records)
STAY IN TUNE WITH MEG PETERSON; A new & revised step by step tuning cassette for the Autoharp & Chromaharp with additional tips
    on instrument care and string changing Meg Peterson Enterprises 1979

KENNY ROGER'S HITS FOR AUTOHARP, Cherry Lane Music Co., 1982

*Cassette Tapes Available